To my love
Anne Marie,
Happy Hauntings!
♡
CFWin

# HAUNTED HOUSE...
# HAUNTED LIFE

**Author's Note**: While some of this short story is based on real events, names and situations have been altered and/or combined to protect the privacy of those involved.

## Chapter 1

In so many towns around the country, families living the proverbial *American Dream* are tucked safely behind white picket fences and meticulously trimmed hedges. The timeline of their lives seems to be at a constant high thanks to forged social media smiles and photo filters—clever tools used to camouflage skeletons buried within the four painted walls of their suburban homes.

But inside every neighborhood there is one house that breaks the cookie cutter mold. The one that kids point at and whisper about. The one they sneak past or dare each other to ding dong ditch. It is the house that can't contain its own drama. Every time its secrets spill out onto the street, the rest of the block watches, horrified but captivated, and completely unaware that they themselves are only one too many glasses of wine and a drunken Facebook post away from being in the spotlight.

Thirty miles outside of New York City, there is a house with a handicap ramp instead of front steps. It sits on land that the Secatogue tribes had roamed before it was settled, divided, and redistributed many times. If not for that ramp, the low ranch with the flower bed next to the driveway might have gone unnoticed. If not for that ramp and why it exists, the house might've only been known as the place where the Parnicello Family starts each day just like everyone else.

Inside the kitchen of that house, Jeanne creeps up behind her husband, Manny. She raises her mug and puts all her strength into the first strike. From that angle, his head jerks forward violently, hurling bits of splintered ceramic into the air and almost propelling his limp body out of the wheelchair.

His flesh tears easily, and his own blood becomes glue for the tufts of hair that have embedded themselves in cracks that fractured and split the base of her cup. More black strands dangle from the rim, now a broken, razor sharp W. The sight of it eggs Jeanne on and fuels her glee.

Manny begs her to stop. She hit him so hard that she can see his bone has been stained red. She continues to beat him, hoping that the sound of her hammering away at his skull will be loud enough to drown out the whining.

*Is today the day?*

*It's not worth it. You'll be gone in a few months. Just breathe and stay cool.*

*After what he's put you through? Get him while he's helpless. Do it.*

Jeanne stuffs her hands under her legs. Instead of acting on her impulses, she stifles her daydream, shifting her eyes from the cup to her spoon, which is turned upside down and dripping coffee into a muddy puddle on the table.

*Don't let the demons control you.*

She knows that once she starts pummeling him, she won't be able to stop. Her husband will be dead, and thanks to her brain cancer, Jeanne will follow right after. But then, instead of getting a well-deserved rest from him and their delinquent sons, she'll be stuck with him for all eternity. In Hell.

*Totally worth it.*

*It's not worth it. Soon you'll be gone. Then he can't bother you anymore. Breathe.*

Jeanne wrestles with herself until she focuses on the voice that seems to have her best interests at heart. Like a mantra doing its job, her muscles start to relax. Although his bloodied head fades, the darker side of her is persistent. It urges her to reconsider but she pushes it away until it's just a vague buzzing sound in the background.

The clock above the sink ticks, supposedly counting down the moments until Jeanne is finally free from the din of a life that was cursed from the beginning. But the hands are stuck—the batteries in the clock are worn down and they struggle to summon enough energy to push the seconds forward.

Jeanne sighs in tired recognition, and watches as the minute hand fights to escape the space between the three and the four. She keeps time with its dying pulse, deliberately tapping the side of her coffee cup with her middle finger.

The sound bothers Manny because when her nail scrapes the ceramic, it mimics some of the bugs that used to chirp outside his bunk—a signal that all was well when he and the other soldiers slept. If the bugs went silent, Manny knew that either the guard was making his rounds, or they were about to be ambushed.

In their kitchen, many years after the war has ended, the fighting is still going on in his head. Jeanne smirks when Manny twitches. He's listening for footsteps; he never rested easily, even though he knew the bugs would warn him.

Her breathing slows, and her mind wanders. Jeanne lights a Parliament and sucks on it deeply, as if it is oxygen.

\*\*\*\*\*

When Jeanne was a little girl, her daddy would talk to the sun. And when the sun went down, he would stay up all night asking the moon and stars questions.

She never saw him with anyone, yet he was never alone. He was often bothered by the attention he got— sometimes looking back at where he had just come from, as if he knew he was being followed, and other times screaming at the clouds to "Shut up! Shut up! Shut up already!"

At first, Jeanne was a silent witness with a jealous curiosity. Although he never acknowledged her, she made herself tiny and hid behind his "collections"—piles of mail, newspapers, and magazines. She wanted a glimpse of who was keeping her father's attention from her. Jeanne watched him whether he was laughing or chasing invisible intruders from the dark corners of their house. Either way, it was painfully obvious that he belonged to a secret club she was not welcome to join.

The older she got, the less she wanted to be a quiet fly on the wall. The moon and the stars eventually revealed her father's disguise and his mystique was stripped. The sun illuminated his schizophrenia in naked, tarnished splendor, his reality now a dark cloud that mocked her.

She would never be "daddy's girl" and he would probably hurt himself. Eventually, someone would find him for the last time. At just ten years old, Jeanne decided that it wouldn't be her.

He was pleading with the sofa as she tiptoed through the cramped living room, carefully escaping to the front door. "I am begging you. Stop haranguing me. I won't do it!"

Jeanne watched him stare vacantly, while his thumb manically traced circles across his other four fingers. She'd seen him do it so many times that she was sure he'd eventually wipe away his own fingerprints.

"You can't fool me," he insisted, shaking his head violently, "I'm supposed to swallow my meds. I'm sure of it. You won't get me to cut open my wrist and drop them into my veins."

He paused as if listening, before defending his stance, "I know it is more efficient, but I can't risk injury. I need to be able to draw and take notes."

Marty looked suspiciously at the pictures hanging above the couch. Jeanne froze, inches from him, when he suddenly reached out. His hand released his meds and the pills scattered like colorful confetti. The arm of his green flannel robe rolled up until the cuff was at his elbow. He was so tall that he could've touched the ceiling, but instead, he poked at the silver frames that sat directly across from his face. The one with Jeanne posing like a model in the blue dress fell to the floor.

He ignored the shards of glass that sliced at his fingers when he reached down and picked up the photo. Marty spoke directly to the little girl in the

picture, her smile now a bloody mess. The little girl
who had just tried on the patent leather Mary Janes she
had been given for her birthday.

She didn't know it then, but it was the last
birthday she'd celebrate with her beloved
grandparents. That same little girl had wriggled into
the blue plaid dress they had bought her the year
before. The dress was too snug around her middle and
it was too short to cover the two inches she had grown,
but she smiled anyway, sucking in her stomach, sure
that her happiness would mask the truth.

Her mother set up the camera, and Jeanne posed,
convinced that these shoes made her as beautiful as the
other little girls in her class. She imagined herself
giggling in tight friend circles on the playground
instead of dodging rocks thrown at her head—the
penalty paid for wearing hand me downs from her
brothers.

All of her excitement disappeared a few hours
later, after Marty sliced up the shoes with hedge
clippers. That day, as Jeanne wailed inconsolably, her
heart aching for the only present she had been
surprised with, her dad spoke into the sink drain, "You
see what I did there? I cut up the shoes, and now Paddy
can't move into them. The nerve! How dare he think
that he can waltz right in and become part of the
family!"

Just two months later, the loss of her shoes would
be reduced to a dull sting in the wake of the car
accident that took her grandparents from her. Everyone
but her father would be shaken to their cores as they
somberly moved their things from their tiny basement

apartment to the upstairs of the home her grandparents
had left them in their will.

Jeanne, now a few years wiser, shuddered
familiarly in the living room, while he yelled at her last
happy memory. "Don't kid yourself," Marty said,
ripping away the shreds of her innocence and opening
old wounds like a dirty bandage clinging to a piece of
fragile skin, "Attachments lead to disappointment,
because the idea of something is always better than the
reality!" He crumpled the picture into a ball and threw
it on the floor, spraying droplets of blood across the
couch as he did.

Although Vivien's voice was muffled behind the
door to her bedroom, it still startled Jeanne every time
she heard it. Her mother's yelling reminded them that
while she wasn't often present, she still lived in their
house. "Shaddup Marty! I'm tryin' ta sleep here!"

Jeanne imagined her mom with her back against
the pillows, taking a long draw on her cigarette and
blowing out the smoke before speaking again.

Jeanne would hold her breath and pray for quiet,
hoping that her mother wouldn't call out for water to
take her Valium. That meant it was a bad day. She
would complain that the water Jeanne brought her was
too warm or that she had been too noisy when she
came in to the room. Without fail, Jeanne would leave,
painfully crying after being punished for her father's
sins.

On a good day, her mother would smash out her
cigarette in the pink ashtray on the nightstand and fall
into an angry silence. She'd study her yellowing
fingernails and veiny hands before sighing and choking

back disappointed tears the same way that Jeanne had seen her do many times.

A few minutes later, the bedroom door slammed open. Vivien pushed past Jeanne just to yell at her husband. "You promised me your best Marty! I don't even know who you are anymore! Where's the guy I fell in love with?"

Jeanne slipped out of the house. She sobbed silently, her pain so intense it might consume her. She let her trembling body release the urine that escaped her underwear and shorts, dripping down her legs and onto the sidewalk outside their house. The wet stain would eventually evaporate but the revealing smell of turmoil would linger until the next rain.

She could hear her parents going at it. Jeanne was still too young to understand why her dad couldn't respond in a way that made sense. Too young to understand why she and her brothers were saddled with a father who could not function in their reality and a mother who had given up on everything.

The window screens at the front of the house were old and worn—as exhausted and neglected as Jeanne's family. Their tiny airholes had finally eroded into gaping peepholes, allowing strangers intimate glimpses into their dysfunction and unhappiness.

Vivien and Marty viciously battered each other, shouting back and forth, like a ping pong match. It was one of the few times her father spoke to someone that Jeanne could see standing in front of him.

Their anger loomed over everyone who lived there, as stagnant and unmoving as the heat on the street where Jeanne crouched. Her hands were flat on the ground next to her, submerged in the yellow puddle that had formed around her feet.

"Marty! Look at what you did! You broke the picture! Why am I surprised? You break everything! Look at how you broke us!"

"You are so loud! You're going to wake them all up with your screeching and I won't have it! You smell of cigarettes and decay. They won't like it!" Marty shot back.

"You smell like shit and crazy, Marty! How do ya like that? You better clean this up and stop breaking things. We're not gonna have a house left!"

Finally, the voices arrived to end the shouting match. "Vivien! Do you understand the importance of what is happening here? Your obsessions are going to be your downfall! The forces that move around on our behalf don't like that. They'll punish you for your wicked thoughts!"

When he was done channeling warnings from his invisible muses, he didn't wait for a response. Instead, Marty walked out of the room, leaving his wife slumped over, her shoulders shuddering rhythmically, keeping time with sobs that she stifled by covering her face with her hands.

Smiling and nodding at something none of them could see, Marty's long, purposeful strides carried him further away from his family, and his attention shifted to the sketch pad he always carried around.

Jeanne tried to peek at that pad whenever she could; it was her only connection to her dad. On it, he drew pictures of what he thought the voices looked like. If they spoke nicely, and one at a time, he called them friends. On paper, he imagined them with smiles and soft lines that Jeanne longed to trace with her finger. But if they screeched obscenities all at once, her father screamed along with them. He'd hold his pencil like a knife and tear at the pages, covering every inch of the once white paper with dark, jagged lines before covering his ears and crouching behind his bed in the extra room. He was so loud that Jeanne or one of her brothers would pull the door shut and turn up the volume on the TV.

*****

Jeanne wishes she could pull a door shut on Manny and his non-stop chattering. He mutters about the war all day long. He whines constantly for things he needs. His sudden bouts of shouting unravel her already frayed nerves.

Now, during a rare moment of silence, he sits across from her at the kitchen table with his own coffee, nursing a marijuana hangover. He says the pot is for pain, but she knows better. He's paralyzed. There's no pain. She's got cancer and he's a tremendous pain in her ass, but she stays away from that stuff.

*Someone's gotta keep a level head when this idiot is high. If not, someone is going to lose an eye...or worse.*

Manny did it to them again last night. It was three in the morning when she woke to the Smith and Wesson trained on her face. At first, she was groggy and confused, having just been jolted out of a dream, but after focusing on the pistol, she came around easily. The last time he had an episode, he had nudged her awake with an M14 rifle, so seeing the smaller gun was almost a relief.

Jeanne pushed the barrel away and sat up, scowling. Having to suffer through his flashbacks was maddening—she would never get used to this—but her resentment grew as she struggled to remember the dream.

In it, she was pushing her best friend, Anna Maria, in a stroller. The thick darkness blocked out any identifying landmarks, but wherever they were, throngs of people milled around them, babbling unintelligibly, sometimes sounding as if their lips were pressed up to Jeanne's ear. Although she and Anna Maria were having fun, shrieks of anguish and deep throated moans overwhelmed them.

"Keep moving," Anna Maria said, "That'll shut them up."

Jeanne obeyed, hitting body after invisible body with the stroller. Painful squeals became an eerie silence, broken only when the two friends giggled wickedly.

"Hey." Manny shoved the gun up against her cheek and the memory was gone. She wanted to yell at him to go away so she could think, but the cold metal distracted her enough to let it all go.

*No matter how many times you get rid of the guns, he finds them! Who keeps giving them back to him?*

Jeanne looked around the room suspiciously, but Manny grew impatient. "Private Jeanne! What the fuck are you doing?! Get outside for roll call!"

*Forget about it. You can't spend all day policing a guy who claims that the weapons protect his family.*

She could hear her sons scrambling in the hallway, no doubt woken up when Manny's commands sliced right through the thin walls of their house. She pictured Anthony and Frank struggling to pull on shoes and race out the front door. If they weren't standing at attention on the front lawn, Manny would pistol whip them and knock them to their knees.

*The boys have time.*

Jeanne still needed to help Manny get out of bed and into his braces. She was a small woman, standing tall at five feet and four inches and weighing in at a skeletal ninety-five pounds. Taking care of a six-foot man who tripled her in mass was slow and unpleasant.

Because of her illness, she bathed him sporadically, so he constantly smelled of urine, body odor, and pot. She held her breath when she got near him, trying hard not to inhale and gag, knowing that the alternative—seeing him naked and atrophied on the regular—was not an option.

Once the braces were on legs that seem to serve no real purpose, he could move quickly and carry multiple items. Sometimes Jeanne caught herself wondering if the paralysis was fake and hating him even more for it.

He screamed obscenities at her the entire time she helped him get ready, the gun decisively aimed at her head. She lifted his dead weight with small, frail arms, and dragged him out of the bed, not confident enough to believe that he wouldn't shoot her one day.

When everyone was there, Manny made them roll around performing army maneuvers while he held them at gunpoint. Somehow, he'd always smuggle an extra weapon out, one in each hand. He kept one carefully trained on Jeanne and forced her to aim another at their sons. His legs weren't working, but his hands were quick—Jeanne and the boys had learned the hard way not to rebel.

The nights had turned cold and they bundled up, knowing that the grass would be wet. But no matter how much they prepared for Manny's sieges, Jeanne and the boys would still suffer discomfort, fear, and embarrassment at the edge of a damaged man's anxiety. Jeanne was sure that the neighborhood judged behind closed doors, over coffee and scrambled eggs, terrified that one day he'd not only unleash all the anguish he'd suffered in battle on his family, but possibly on the rest of the block.

Last night, Manny was particularly loud when he chased them outside, and a sleepy crowd formed across the street. As they crept toward the scene, they kept a safe distance, leaving plenty of room to dive or run.

Jeanne saw Manny cock his head like he was listening for something. "They're coming, I can sense it, and none of you recruits is ready to defend your country! Get to your feet! Now!"

The noisy pain in her head had been so bad that she wanted to take one of Manny's guns and blast open her skull herself, to let out whatever was banging on it. As she stood up slowly, conserving just enough energy to jolt forward and startle Manny into shooting her without thinking, she glanced at the porch and remembered that she wasn't ready to die yet. She still had some searching to do. After that, the brain tumor or Manny could kill her; it would just be a matter of whose trigger finger was faster. Until then, Jeanne did as she was told, even though it would be another twenty minutes until Manny regained his mind and let them go back inside.

The house, a modest low ranch in middle class suburbia, was built for the disabled veteran and paid for by several government grants the family finagled because of his injuries. He had been shot in Vietnam and was now stuck in a wheelchair—although his wife suspected that someone in his platoon had gotten sick of him and tried to kill him just to find peace while at war. She was still pissed off that there weren't better gun training classes.

*Manny is huge. How hard could it have been to spare us all by hitting the right spot and finishing the job?*

They built a house with large rooms, and an oversized hallway—whatever it took to make Manny comfortable—but he was still cranky and unstable. And despite his limitations, he was feared.

*He can't lift a finger to help around the house, but chaos?—that he's good at.*

Now, the morning after, Jeanne is faced with the knowledge that last night was not a dream. That she shares a space with the damaged shell of a worthless human being she is legally bound to call her husband. Her stomach jolts with regret and her heart aches as her will to live fades.

She sips her coffee and stares at Manny, wishing

she could go back and rewrite her life. She and Anna Maria had discussed the possibility of time travel many times, but neither had enough knowledge or education in science and math to make it happen.

Jeanne misses Anna Maria so much that her chest hurts. She lets her thoughts slip back again, desperate to remember how they had become friends.

*Be patient and wade through the pain. Bit by bit, it will come back to you. Follow the pieces like breadcrumbs, and they will lead you to her.*

\*\*\*\*\*

Soon after one of his kids shut the bedroom door, Marty would stop yelling. Even so, the silence that followed would be louder than their TV program. Eventually, her brothers would send Jeanne in to make sure Marty hadn't hurt himself.

Jeanne hated doing it, but she went anyway, absentmindedly rubbing the bruises that hadn't yet healed from the last time she resisted the boys' commands. They had hit and pinched her, unwilling to admit that they wanted to remember their father as a fun loving, gentle man. As the man who had once put his sons on his knees and bounced them up and down like they were riding a horse.

By the time Jeanne was born, Marty was disappearing. He took with him the love that had drawn her parents together and urged them to start a family. When Jeanne clawed her way out of her mother's womb, she screeched desperately, as if begging her dad to stay.

Her constant wailing pierced their ears. "Vivien, you really should just consider killing this pig and serving it for Easter. You've done a good job of fattening it up. It's time." He poked at Jeanne's thigh while Vivien tried unsuccessfully to get her to latch to her breast.

Each day, Marty withdrew more and more, until he finally morphed into some random guy who talked to himself and lived in their house.

Jeanne pushed open the bedroom door a tiny bit. She held her breath and stood on her tiptoes, so she could see the top of Marty's head. He was sitting on the floor, his back against the far side of the bed. If his hair twitched, she knew he was alive and pulling out a clean sheet of paper from his pad. Jeanne's heart pounded hard. She snuck all the way around till she faced him.

Marty wouldn't let anyone get close enough to help bathe or groom him. The dark pieces of hair that he hacked away at with a steak knife stood straight up, not long enough to cover the bald spots from where he had yanked it out at the root.

His teeth, once polished white, were now yellow and beginning to rot. "I can't use this stuff!" Marty threw the tube of toothpaste on the floor. It clattered against the tiles and rolled toward the tub while he scrubbed his hands with soap.

"The devil hides himself in the peppermint because it smells nice. It entices all of you sheep to put it in your mouth. Once its minty goodness hits your taste buds, it's too late." He explained it loudly to the lightbulb above his head.

"By then, Beelzebub has entered the body and taken over the soul. By then, you are doomed." Jeanne was crouched behind a stack of National Geographic magazines just outside the door, watching and listening.

Sometimes she would hesitate at the sink with her brush in front of her mouth. *What if Marty knows something you don't? What if he's not the crazy one?* As soon as her brothers pounded on the bathroom door and screamed for her to hurry up, the doubting voice crept back into the recesses of her mind.

On the floor next to his bed, Marty was bent so close to the paper that his face took on a white glow. He wouldn't look up, even if the floorboards creaked under Jeanne's feet.

Thick slashes of blues and blacks covered the page; Marty pushed his pen so hard that he almost ripped right through. He ignored Jeanne, chuckling and muttering the whole time he recreated his version of the evil that his friends had become. "Trapping you. Can't get out of this now…"

Before her grandparents died, Jeanne had listened to hushed conversations, piecing together some explanation of why her dad was the way he was.

Everyone agreed. "He had such promise." Her grandmother rubbed Vivien's head.

"With the proper care…" Her grandfather's voice trailed off helplessly.

When Vivien still had friends, they stopped by with casserole dishes and curious eyes that gave away the insincerity of all the right words they used to feign concern.

Marty paced back and forth behind them, quietly muttering. Suddenly he screamed, "If you don't stop talking about me, I'm going to kill you all!"

At that time, Jeanne was still small enough to fit in a cabinet. She was careful not to knock over the ammonia bottles next to her as she cracked open the door. She watched her parents' friends hastily gather their coats and leave.

"He doesn't mean you," Vivien called after them, "He hears voices. He means he's gonna kill them, not you."

Their friends nodded and kissed her cheek, every one of them promising to check on her. Except for a few bundt cakes left on the stoop for a week or two, everyone stopped coming.

Marty was a well-educated artist; an intelligent man who could draw, paint, and sculpt, with offers from galleries all over the world to show his work. When they were still young and naïve, he and Vivien would dream over celebratory dinners.

"This is it, Marty. If the Soho Gallery showing is a success, this will be your big break," Vivien said, as she poured glasses of milk for their sons. "Everyone says they are coming, and your agent thinks there will be a lot of buyers there."

Marty made a hole in the middle of his mashed potatoes and filled it with gravy. "Yeah, Viv. It's happening for us."

He scowled and added another spoonful of potatoes, carefully spreading them out in a thin circle. He filled the space between the pile and the circle with more gravy. "You gettin' inspired by the mashed potatoes Marty?" Vivien laughed. "You artists. I could never think the way you do."

"Ssh!" Marty said. He leaned his face close to the plate and stared at his gravy castle and moat. When he suddenly stabbed at the food and muttered, "That's no good. No good at all," Vivien's face fell. He shoveled the potatoes into his mouth. "I'll eat you before I let you get to her and my baby."

Over the next few months, he began compiling pieces, only to later destroy them, complaining that the "critics" had panned his creations and called him a "no-talent hack".

Vivien clutched her growing belly and cried. "What critics Marty? Nobody's seen your stuff yet!"

They lost their apartment after he stacked all his paintings in the living room and soaked them with four bottles of cooking oil. Vivien found him in the kitchen with their boys. They were loading marshmallows on forks just as the curtains caught fire.

"Marty! What are you doing'?" She grabbed her sons, one in each hand and ran out the door.

Marty trailed behind them, awkwardly shuffling down two flights of stairs. The sirens from the fire trucks were so loud as they pulled up to the curb that they almost drowned out Marty's babbling. "You're all going down," he said. "Burn in hell, Harry. They'll find your charred remains because I won't tell them you're in there," he said to no one.

Several firemen armed with axes pushed past Vivien's swollen belly before one stopped. "Is anyone else up there, ma'am?"

"No," Vivien said dully, shaking her head. She

held her sons' hands tightly and let the tears flow. For the loss of her husband's sanity. For all of the photos and love notes that the fire would destroy. They were the only evidence of how things had once been normal, and she had been happy.

After they moved in with Vivien's parents, Marty struggled to function in a world that he complained would change whenever he finally felt comfortable. "Viv! Stop moving things around! The salt shaker is at an angle that makes it easy for the ants to get in! To form an army!"

Vivien sighed and took the salt off the table. She put it in the cabinet over the stove and said, "Don't you have to get ready for work?"

Marty made very little money as a house painter, only sometimes picking up odd jobs as a fine artist if someone wanted a mural done in their child's room. He would whistle softly as he sketched out a sleepy underwater scene, taking care to draw the sea creatures' eyes half closed so they couldn't spy on him.

For a while, he fought an invisible war to protect his family. To stay with them. His sense of responsibility wrestled with his mental illness. He resisted its charms for as long as he could, keeping control by day and reserving his meltdowns for his family at night.

Eventually, he grew tired, deteriorating into someone his family didn't recognize. Marty would sit at the table for hours, studying a glass of milk, looking for signs meant only for him. The more it curdled, the more fixated he became.

Vivien tsk'd softly and shook her head, her resentment growing with every gasp he released. Marty's head moved back and forth, as if following a pesky fly. Vivien banged the table to get his attention. "Marty! Look at me!"

He ignored her before complaining in a suspicious man's whisper, "They are always listening to our conversations. They can hear my thoughts!"

Vivien reached for a cigarette. "How can you say that? My parents wouldn't stoop so low! And even if they could hear us all the way upstairs, they'd get bored! Who wants to listen to us talk about not having any money?"

Marty cocked his head. He seemed lost in thought until he pointed at his wife and shouted. "Are you telling them? Sometimes they let things slip. They think I don't hear them, but I do. Your name keeps coming up. Explain yourself!"

These outbursts always ended the same way— with Vivien crying, something broken, and Marty disappearing. By the time he came back, he looked like he had slept under a bridge.

When he walked in the door, Vivien didn't run and hug him. Instead, she took a cigarette from the pack and lit it. "Marty! Where the hell have you been? You left me here to take care of the kids all by myself for two days! Are you cheating on me?"

He lifted an eyebrow. "I've been here the whole time, Vivien! Are you off your rocker? We just spent the day in the park with Louis!" He pointed at the high chair in the corner where baby Jeanne was eating spaghetti with her fingers. Her older brothers sat at the kitchen table coloring.

A leaf fell off Marty's vest and they all watched it fall on the floor. He picked it up and held out the evidence. "Do you see this, Vivien? It's from the *park*! P—A—R—K – *Park!*"

Finally, everything came to a head on the last day he was painting the Geiger's house. On the day the voices told him that he could be more. "You can save the world, Marty," they said.

The ones he called Fitz and Craig whispered above the rest of the voices, who chattered away in tongues. Over the years, Jeanne and her family would come to know Fitz and Craig. They would cringe every time Marty called out to them for advice or comfort, but especially when he screamed in terror over the hold they had on him.

When Fitz and Craig spoke, the others faded quickly into the background, deferring to the voices that were clearly in charge and most influential when it came to getting Marty to do what they wanted.

That last day on the job, Fitz and Craig shushed the others and counseled him. "We can protect this family from all the evil in the world if you design a mosaic of our eyes. That way we can watch over them and keep them safe. Do it on the south wall of the living room."

While the Geigers were at school and work, Marty created each eye in painstaking detail, made exactly as it was described to him on that Thursday afternoon. He nodded as he painted, blending browns and greens and adding flecks of yellow. Never questioning, only listening and doing as he was told.

Their guardians came alive on the sheetrock, so
life-like that when the horrified family finally stood in
front of it, the youngest Geiger screamed, "The red
one! The one that's bloodshot and oozing pus! It just
winked at me!"

The teenager's loud fear blended easily with the
shrieking in Marty's head. He ignored the noise and
admired his work—a piece of art that collectors
would've fought over if given the chance to view it.
But after Marty was fired, his efforts and expertise
were erased, easily returned to a plain eggshell wall,
the promise of a successful life overhauled with the
simple stroke of a paintbrush.

Unemployed and unwilling to abandon his art,
Marty muttered and paced their tiny basement
apartment. Vivien, exhausted and struggling to care for
three small children, had no idea what to do, now that
her husband had left them.

*****

"Why do you do that? You know I'm sitting here,
helpless all day long, but when I ask you to get me
some milk for my coffee, it's the hardest thing in the
world for you to answer me. To acknowledge that I'm
speaking." Manny slurs his words, jarring Jeanne out
of her childhood trauma and thrusting her into the daily
torture she endures with him.

*If only you could find her, you'd die in peace.*

Jeanne feels the pull of that statement but
dismisses it. Instead, she tears her eyes away from the
window—the one with the bullet hole—and scowls at

Manny. "Maybe I didn't hear you. I've got stuff on my mind too ya know. I've *literally* got stuff on my mind—like the tumor that's wrapped itself around my brain. And death. What's your biggest worry?"

She holds her hands to her sunken cheeks, mimicking a scared face. She almost knocks her wig off her head, but she doesn't push the thin wisps of blond hair back up into hiding. Instead, they stick out, the last tufts of what the hairdresser had called a thick mane. Once healthy, bouncy, and full of life, it had almost disappeared, dying a slow death alongside her deteriorating brain cells.

Manny turns his wheelchair away from her, toward the damaged window, as if not looking at her is the same as not hearing her.

She taunts him in an exaggerated, high-pitched voice. "Oh no! I sharted! Who's gonna change my diaper and clean me up?"

Manny's silence fuels Jeanne's anger after being forced out onto the lawn last night. "Oh, did I hurt your wittle feelings?! That's ok. Turn away and admire the lovely view you made for all of us to see every time we sit here trying to enjoy a meal."

She spits out jabs, ignoring the drool dripping from her chin. "Did you think it was funny when the cops stormed the house? After you decided to shoot at someone through the glass just because they were walking by? Thank God the only casualty that day was the window!"

Suddenly, she is on her feet, pointing at him, the floodgates flung open. "I can't believe they took pity on you and didn't arrest you! What kind of legal system do we have in this town anyway? Everybody was talking about it, ya know. But because you're too gimpy to leave the house, they had to stare at your poor, sick wife, all the while wondering why she stays with such a crazy, useless, piece of shit!"

By then, Jeanne is screeching, the pain in her head intense enough to throw her off balance. She collapses back into the chair, panting and grabbing for her seizure meds.

*Get it together Jeanne. That woman is coming to see the house today. You'd better keep looking. The clock's ticking.*

Her breathing slows, but her eyes glaze over as she fades back into the past again.

*You're almost there. If you play it out, you'll remember your first day with her. If you can picture her face and read her lips, she'll tell you where she is.*

\*\*\*\*\*

By the time Jeanne was born, her parents had just about given up on their collective sanity, so she grew up never knowing what love looked like. As a small child, she'd climb into her mother's lap hoping to snuggle, but instead, she'd be pushed to the floor. "Mama! Mama! the kids at school threw rocks at me," she cried, clinging so tightly to Vivien's legs that it took three tries to kick her away.

"I...just..can't. Your Mama's tired."

Sometimes Jeanne watched her father. She approached him slowly, so as not to startle him. Often animated and unpredictable, Jeanne's dad was

animated and unpredictable, Jeanne's dad was a
science project, something to be observed and studied
from a safe distance. Her palms were sweaty, but she
was eager to shake hands with his invisible friends.

He said he couldn't see who was talking, that they
always stood behind him, leaning on his shoulder and
yammering away in his ear. Jeanne squinted her eyes,
straining not just to see or hear something, but hoping
to be noticed and eventually invited to join in.

Marty looked past her. "Fitz! Craig! The
negativity is suffocating me! Do something quick! The
blackness of it all is overwhelming!"

While Marty fought to stay alive in their home,
Jeanne struggled at school. She was the poor kid with
the crazy parents. She was the weirdo who daydreamed
and babbled to herself. The one who carried on loudly
enough to be heard over the class as they recited their
times tables. At recess, the other girls mocked her
magic marker painted nails and the boys poked her
with pencils.

When Jeanne was old enough to realize she
would never matter as much as her parents' problems
did but was still young enough to be wounded by the
truth, she began thinking of them as Marty and Vivien
instead of Mom and Dad.

*Moms and dads hug and kiss their children. They
tuck them in at night. You live with strangers—two
broken people, unfit to have kids.*

Jeanne couldn't find acceptance with her family
and was convinced that the rest of the world saw her in
the same way—useless and nonexistent. Even if she
had been able to make a friend, she was not allowed to

invite anyone over to play. Her tiny fingers were crossed and her eyes hopeful when she begged her mother to allow it.

"Why are you always nagging me?" Her mother complained as she opened a fresh pack of cigarettes. When Vivien smoked her Parliaments, she would turn her head and blow huge clouds of smoke toward the open window, away from Jeanne, one small revealing act of affection.

"I've told you a hundred times. Your dad can't handle you and your friends running around like wild animals. It makes him nervous. What the hell is wrong with you that you can't see that?"

Jeanne always did the same thing when her mother yelled at her. She uncrossed her fingers and folded her hands in her lap, praying silently that one day someone might like her.

*I just need one friend. If one person at school would eat lunch with me, then I wouldn't care when the other kids trip me or make fun of my family. Please God. Please do this one thing for me.*

"Okay now, look what you did. You gave me a splitting headache. I gotta lay down." Vivien sighed when she stood up. She used the table for support, as if the weight of the world was pressing against her. She poked out the stub of her cigarette in the ashtray she had made from the bottom of an aluminum can.

"Listen, Jeanne, you're gonna have to understand that friends don't last anyways." Vivien's voice softened. She followed her mother's eyes. Marty was pacing back and forth in the spare room across from them.

They watched him as Vivien lit another cigarette. The action had become as natural as eating, a habit Jeanne would eventually pick up when she too decided that nicotine was comfort food.

Marty waved his hands excitedly above his head. One held his mechanical pencil. He used it to draw figure eights in the air as he stalked from one side of the room to the other.

Vivien kept her eyes on him while she spoke to Jeanne between long draws on her Parliament. "When you're young, you think that things are great and that it'll last forever, but life is a bitch. She can't stand to see you happy, so she ambushes you just when you relax because you think it's all ok. It never is, and the sooner you learn to depend on yourself, the better."

Vivien sighed and shook her head. This time, when her mother exhaled, the smoke landed right in Jeanne's face, proving that Vivien was right—nothing lasts forever, not even the tiniest maternal instinct. The filmy smoke imprinted on Jeanne as soon as she breathed it in. It became part of her, even more so than her memories would.

"You don't get to pick your family either. Not that it matters 'cause they're always a buncha disappointments too," Vivien said, with one more glance in Marty's direction.

Suddenly, she tsk'd loudly and thumped the table with her fist. "What's with the tears, Jeanne? What?"

Marty yelled from the other room, "Vivi! Get in the cellar! God is sending the locusts! The storms, Vivien!" He slammed the door shut.

Then the house was silent except for Jeanne's

heaving sobs. Her brothers were out riding their bikes. When she called for them, her mother's shrill voice echoed throughout the neighborhood, but Jeanne knew that they took their time coming home for the night.

Vivien rubbed her head and squeezed her eyes shut. "Yeah. I understand. You're lonely, huh? Fine. Shuddup. Just shuddup, Jeanne. Lemme think."

Her mother walked into the long hallway, leaving a smoke trail behind her as her slippers slapped the wood floor. Jeanne's crying slowed.

Vivien opened the second door on the right, the junk closet, a place that Jeanne and her brothers were never allowed to open or poke through. She tried to creep closer and take a peek, but her mother swatted at her, warning her to get back in the kitchen. Vivien dug around for a few minutes, letting the cigarette dangle from her mouth and squinting when the smoke drifted into her eyes.

"Yeah, yeah, here it is", she mumbled, barely audible over the angry conversation Marty was now having with the rug in the other room. The ashes from her cigarette, almost two inches long, finally fell to the floor, unnoticed.

Jeanne's tears left damp streaks on her cheeks. Their trails ended at an unsure smile that shook slightly when she saw what her mother was holding. Vivien tossed it on the table in front of her before she turned her back on them both.

"Her name is Anna Maria. She can be your friend," her mom said as she trudged to her bedroom and banged the door shut.

Anna Maria landed face down on the floral

placemat in front of Marty's seat. Jeanne looked around before reaching out to pick her up. *What if this is another mean joke, like when Peter Miller pulled your chair out from under you at school?*

When no one jumped out to push her away and snatch the doll, she picked her up gently. She stared at Anna Maria's blond hair and blue eyes. Her plaid dress was a perfect fit for her slim body, and her petite feet sat arched and ready for high heels, even though she wore cute flats. The penny loafers were the same ones that Jeanne had begged for many times before her mother slapped her and told her to, "Shuddup already!"

Anna Maria was everything that Jeanne wished she herself could be. As she stroked the doll's cheeks, she was sure that she saw her pink lips quiver.

*She's trying to talk.*

"There, there, Anna Maria. You'll be able to tell me everything before you know it. Soon we'll whisper all our secrets to each other. We don't need anyone else."

She went with Jeanne to school and slept next to her every night. Now that she had someone to talk to, Jeanne stopped caring about what the other kids thought. When they taunted her, or slammed her books to the ground, Anna Maria was quick to counsel her about how to handle the situation.

*Mary the Miserable is a fat cow. Pee into a jar and then dump it in her locker through the little slits on the top of the door.*

When it was done, Jeanne held the doll up so that she could see too. The halls were empty at four in the afternoon, so there was no one there to catch them in the act. They stared at the wet streaks on the outside of Mary's locker and giggled, ignoring the smell of urine on Jeanne's hands.

*School dances are for robot kids who take orders. Don't go, Jeanne. You'll wake up and realize that you're one of them after it's too late, when you're about to follow them off the edge of a cliff. Instead, we'll stay home and glue your nasty brothers' fingers together when they're asleep.*

While her classmates spent the night wearing fancy clothes and dancing, Jeanne had the time of her life with her only friend. "Anna Maria, you saved me. I love our adventures and all the stuff you teach me. You're my best friend. I don't know what I'd do without you."

*Without me, the evil in the world would smother you. I make you strong enough to rise above it.*

In only a few short years, her mother would try to destroy her happiness. "I know what you did Jeanne." Vivien muttered and held the lighter close to Anna Maria's smiling face. "You took my cigarettes for yourself and now you're gonna tell me the doll told you to do it."

Her braids caught fire easily. The braids Jeanne had made for Anna Maria between puffs on Vivien's cigarettes. The smoke had lazily wafted up between them and out Jeanne's bedroom window.

"Time to grow up. The doll's gotta go!"

The synthetic materials that gave Jeanne's only friend her form created a toxic cloud above Anna Maria's head as they began to melt away. The cloud was dark and heavy, like the one that had been hanging over their family for as long as she could remember. Its smell was as acrid as the life they had been forced into. Jeanne was seventeen years old when she snatched the doll from her mother. When Vivien was overtaken by a hacking cough that had attached itself to her lungs. It had lingered, eternally devoted to her in the absence of family and friends.

She pushed Vivien to the floor and ran with Anna Maria to the kitchen sink, where she plunged her head under the faucet. Vivien writhed on the floor, choking on her own phlegm. Jeanne yelled, "You're a monster! Don't ever put your hands on her again!"

When the flames were out, she stood over her mother and smothered Anna Maria with kisses. Vivien grabbed Jeanne's leg and pleaded between raspy breaths for her to call the doctor, but it was Jeanne's turn to kick her off. She left her to suffer alone, happily closing her bedroom door on Vivien's whimpering. She giggled and chatted with Anna Maria before carefully tucking her in for the night.

Sometime in the wee hours, between his usual routine of pacing and babbling, Marty came into Jeanne's room—something he had never done before—and plucked Anna Maria from her soft cardboard bed.

He spoke to the doll softly, nodding and smiling as he brushed and dabbed at her with putty and one of his paint brushes. He refurbished her skin per Anna Maria's instructions—she had always admired the stark white appearance of the ladies of the Renaissance era. Then he painted a burlesque-like mouth over her charred pink lips.

When he woke Jeanne to show her, she blinked twice before she realized she wasn't dreaming. It was the only time she could remember her father talking directly to her instead of looking past her as if she were invisible.

"There you go. Your friend is pretty again. She says she was ready for a change anyway."

Jeanne stared wide-eyed. She trembled when she took the doll from Marty, but she nodded. "You're right Daddy. Thank you."

Marty studied the space above his daughter's head for a second, then stormed off, shouting at Fitz to keep his voice down. "The inmates will riot if they don't sleep, Fitz! Shut your trap! That's an order!"

Jeanne held Anna Maria tightly. Marty's ranting was static noise behind the one voice that truly mattered. *Don't let them separate us, Jeanne. I know you better than you know yourself. Without me, you won't survive.*

Jeanne nodded and whispered the same promise she'd recited so many times. Now though, after what her mother had done, the promise meant so much more. "Anna Maria, I'll never let you go. We will always be together."

She smiled when they found Vivien dead the next morning—still sprawled out on the kitchen floor, amongst a pile of unlit cigarettes that had fallen out of the pack she always kept in her housecoat pocket.

Jeanne held her doll to her ear and listened. *You see that? We're a great team. Another mess all cleaned up.*

When Jeanne turned back to the corpse, she

thought of how her mother had always been an empty, lifeless shell. She seemed no less animated lying on the floor in a heap than she did when she locked herself away in her bedroom.

Blank faced and pitiless, Jeanne vowed to live a better life. She stroked her doll and let her obsession grow. "I'll never let you go. We will always be together."

After her father was finally institutionalized, locked in a padded cell with only the voices for company, Jeanne's attachment intensified. "Anna Maria, you have always been so loyal, please don't ever leave me. Stay and we will always be together."

A few years later, she married the first man who paid any attention to her. Manny was amused by Jeanne's quirky fixation on the doll. He humored her when she insisted that Anna Maria be her maid of honor at their wedding.

Her preoccupation with the doll would be strengthened whenever he indulged their friendship, but more so when he challenged it. Jeanne shot him down with scathing insults she and Anna Maria had practiced. Then, late at night, with their heads close together, Jeanne confided in her friend, "Don't worry. No man will ever come between us. We will always be together."

As her mother passed out for the last time, as she watched her father being loaded into an ambulance, and a few minutes after she said her vows, Jeanne's devotion to her best friend deepened. Each time she swore to prove her mother wrong. "Anna Maria, I'll never let you go. We will always be together."

# Chapter 2

Thirty miserable years later, Jeanne is tossing the contents of her dresser drawers. Although they have lived in this house for almost a decade, Jeanne wants to die in Florida, with the family members that took her in after her mother passed away. The doctors can't give her a more precise ETD than *by the end of the year,* so the Parnicellos know that the sooner they move, the better.

Jeanne wants to be buried with Anna Maria—her confidante when Manny came home from the war both physically and mentally damaged, and her therapist when she was diagnosed with brain cancer. But she doesn't know where she hid her after she put twenty thousand dollars in the doll's head. She was afraid that Manny or the boys would find the money, so she gave it to the one she trusts the most, for safe keeping.

*If those lazy sons of bitches find out about it, they'll take it for themselves and buy drugs.*

Because of all the veteran grants Manny had gotten, they had saved on the construction of their house. When real estate prices jumped, right after her diagnosis, Jeanne took out a second mortgage and withdrew the cash. The money is meant for Trish, her niece and the single mother of two small children.

Manny was high the day he signed the papers she laid out on the table in front of him. "Print, sign, and initial right here, Manny." Jeanne handed him a pen and he unknowingly cosigned her bank loan. "We need to make sure that you have Power of Attorney over everything when I am too sick to manage it anymore."

She had smirked when she took the documents and put them in a folder.

*As if he can be trusted with anything more than the TV remote.*

The sicker she gets, the fuzzier her memory becomes. Searching for the doll is now part of her daily routine. "Where, Jeanne? Where did you put her?" She mumbles to herself while she paces back and forth, rifling through drawers and closets.

*Once you get the money out, you can deposit it and send a check to Trish's new house. The surprise will make Trish forget about her bad luck with men. You can die knowing that you did a good deed, and she'll make sure that you're buried with Anna Maria.*

*But what about dinner?*

"Oh yeah. That's right. I need to make a grocery list." Jeanne leaves the pile of sweaters on the floor and goes to the kitchen to get a piece of paper and something to write with. Later, she'll find the clothes and forget that she emptied the dresser to look for the doll. Instead she'll fold everything up, thinking that it's laundry that needs to be put away.

The tumor distracts her as it strangles her cells and drains her life force. Tomorrow, she'll begin looking for Anna Maria in the same place, never making it to the sewing room where the doll is.

When her son Frank was a teen, and before the motorcycle crash in California that got him addicted to pain meds, the sewing room was his bedroom. Hopped up on hormones, he cut a square out of the wall behind the dresser and created the perfect hiding spot for his porn. Now, Anna Maria lies among stained, tattered pictures of tits and ads for hi tech dildos, patiently waiting to be rescued.

At two o'clock Jeanne hears voices in the front yard. She sizes up the potential buyer for her house as she and the realtor make their way along the driveway. *Prego is waddling a little more slowly than she should be.*

The woman shakes her head and stops walking. Jeanne sees her grab the realtor by the arm. Their voices are muffled, so Jeanne quietly inches her window up and leans toward the screen.

"This house looks kind of small," the woman says. Jeanne balls her hands up into fists when the woman points toward the door. "And look at this rickety handicap ramp! The listing said it was a wrap-around porch! I've seen enough dumps for one day. Can we just go?"

Jeanne's face is hot when she steps back from the window and finds her Parliaments. She stares, willing them to continue into the house as she sucks on the freshly lit cigarette. *Is she kidding?*

"This is the last stop for today. Let's just give it a chance." Her realtor convinces her. The woman steps gingerly onto the ramp and follows it to the front door. She lets her escort ring the bell.

Jeanne straightens her wig and angrily stabs out the cigarette in the ashtray on the window sill. *That bitch doesn't like people smoking around her belly. She's one of those.*

"The door!" Manny calls out to her like she's the butler.

She wants to yell back, "Die!" but they'll

probably hear her and run. Instead, she smiles and lets them in, never realizing that her emaciated body and decaying teeth are probably more terrifying than them hearing her feud with her husband.

As soon as the woman crosses the threshold, Jeanne sees her face change. *She's happily surprised— as she should be.*

Jeanne knows that the house is bigger than it appears from the outside. The few that have dared to visit nickname it the *Alice In Wonderland House* because of the deception...and probably the lingering smell of drugs that she attempts to cover up with fresh flowers and Glade.

The woman speaks to the realtor, "It's so nice to be able to move around normally! Did you notice me in the last house? It was so tight that I had to walk sideways as I went from room to room."

*At least this hallway is wide enough for Manny's wheelchair AND the second baby she's carrying in her ass.*

The women shake hands, and the buyer speaks excitedly. "Hi. I'm Catherine. I have to tell you... as soon as I stepped in, it was like all of the space rushed at me and hit me in the face—but in a good way. This is so different than I thought it would be."

Jeanne smiles—sincerely this time—and says, "C'mon in and let me show you the rest of it."

She takes her through the master bedroom and bath and the two smaller bedrooms and bathroom that make up the long hallway. Then Jeanne leads the way to the living room and kitchen at the back of the house. There are cathedral ceilings, skylights, and wood floors that Catherine gushes over. The extra-large sliding glass door in the kitchen opens up onto a deck which overlooks a huge backyard.

She asks, "What is the property size?"

"It's about a quarter acre," the realtor answers.

"I have two other children," Catherine explains, while patting her belly. "I'd love to put a swing set in the corner of the yard for them to play on."

Jeanne tries to see the house through Catherine's eyes. If she can overlook the yellow tobacco stains on all of the walls and windows, it's a pretty house with a huge amount of property.

*In fact, for the price, it's a steal. Are we asking for too little?*

"Let's see the second floor," Catherine says enthusiastically. She turns from the backyard and walks toward a door in the living room. It leads to the unfinished, dirty basement where racial slurs are spray painted on the concrete walls, left there after a drug filled fiesta that Jeanne's sons and their friends organized. Jeanne had frowned when she went downstairs to do laundry and saw it.

*The apple doesn't fall far from the tree. And their apples are all filled with heroin.*

Jeanne swats the air as if a bug is buzzing around her ear. "There is no second floor," she says, hoping that Catherine is too far along in her pregnancy to want to tackle the stairs and see *The Den Of Shame*.

Catherine's disappointed smile reveals that she's hooked and wants more. "I'll take it!"

A few days after they close on the house, Jeanne and her tribe move to Florida, leaving behind a fridge full of spoiling food and several urine bottles—turned fluorescent green from meds and hanging in the bathroom.

\*\*\*\*\*

In the weeks that follow, Catherine and her two young children take their time hauling in boxes and bags, excited to start their new life in their new home. After Catherine gives birth to her youngest, a second girl, they'll transfer all of their belongings over. Then they won't be living out of two rooms in her mother's house anymore.

"Mama!" Rebecca yells, "I want this room!" She is standing in the doorway, straddling the bigger bedroom and the hallway, as if staking her claim. Catherine nods and laughs, giving her oldest child permission to choose first.

The kids slide down the long, wide hallway on their knees, laughing and squealing before pulling open the back door and bounding down the deck stairs onto the soft grass of their massive backyard. They chase each other and jump around like the crickets they hear at night.

As part of the deal, the Parnicellos have thrown in some pieces of mismatched living room furniture. Catherine is thrilled since she hasn't bought beds yet. Until then, she and Rebecca will sleep on the couches.

She hires a service to clean and disinfect the hand me down furniture. Catherine is rolling up the area rug in the living room when she cries out. "Oh my God. What is that?" She and the technician stare at the patch of hardwood floor that was hidden by both the rug and couch that sat on top of it. It looks like a large lily pad and smells like the urine that ate away at the wood.

Adam comes bounding in from outside. Catherine yells when he squats, his intention to leap into the dark spot. "No Adam!" She grabs him around the waist, scooping him up and tucking him under her armpit like a football. He ribbits at her. "No honey. Frogs jump on green lily pads, not pee pads!"

Rebecca, the oldest, giggles. "Mommy! You said pee!"

Catherine laughs weakly, feeling like she's just been duped. She imagines Manny, high and unaware of what room he was in, watching TV when he opened his zipper and let himself go all over the floor.

"Oh boy," the technician says, "You want a referral? I know somebody who's good with floors. No guarantees that he'll get the whole thing, but if you want his number..."

Catherine nods, adding the floor repair to the top of her list, a priority before she replaces the window pane in the kitchen.

She sighs, only mildly wishing she wasn't single. The moment passes quickly when she reminds herself that although she could use a little help and some extra income, the father of her children has proven to be useless.

In a few years, she will discover that he has a wife and two more children in another town, and the only comfort about being the unsuspecting victim of her own dramatic TV mini-series will be knowing that she is not legally bound to him. Catherine continues prepping the house for their move in, determined to give her kids a normal life.

A few weeks later, she puts her key in the lock. "Ok you guys. Hold hands. When I count to three, jump into the house. I'll be right behind you with baby Maya."

It is *move in and stay put* day. Catherine strokes her newborn, asleep in a Snuggie, cradled in the warmth of her mother's body and watchful eye.

She smiles when Rebecca and Adam hop across the threshold. "This is it. New house, new life."

Rebecca and Adam cheer loudly, then run into their rooms to grab some toys. Maya stirs slightly before falling back to sleep. Catherine steps in, her own excitement obvious in the way she laughs when she closes the front door.

They still don't have beds to sleep on, so Catherine converts the living room into one big bedroom. She and Rebecca camp out on the couches, Adam snoozes on a soft blanket in his playpen, and Maya stays in her car seat next to her mother, waking every three hours to feed and cuddle.

During the day, everyone is home—Catherine is on maternity leave, and the kids are not due to start preschool and Kindergarten till the fall. They spend lots of time together, enjoying the space both inside and outside the house.

"Mommy." Rebecca stands in the kitchen, frowning, one hand on her hip and the other holding her favorite Barbie doll. Its evening gown is hanging from one arm, but the hair is brushed, styled and ready for a night on the town. "Why was Charlotte on the floor in the living room?"

Catherine pulls the screen door shut and faces her daughter. She picks a piece of grass from Rebecca's hair, probably carried in after Rebecca grabbed her brother during a game of tag and rolled around with him on the ground. Adam had giggled hysterically when she tickled him.

She is amazed at how quickly children's attention can shift from one activity to another. "Maybe Adam was playing with it and left it there. He's only one year old, so he's not very good at putting things away yet."

She walks away from her daughter, down the hallway with the baby, who needs a new diaper. "Hey Monkey. Are you ready to get all fresh and clean?" Catherine kisses Maya's forehead. "Yes, you are. Look at that smile." She's sure that this child came out of the womb already knowing the secret to happiness.

Catherine hears Rebecca stalk off, calling out for her brother. She leans back while she reaches for the wipes, so that she is close to the door. Then she can see and hear the conversation.

Rebecca takes Adam by the hand, leading him to the living room. He toddles along willingly, his adoration for both of his sisters always obvious in his grin and easy going demeanor. She sits him down on the loveseat and stands in front of him.

"Adam, look at me." Her brother smiles, then hides his face in his hands.

"No Adam, look at me. I'm not playing peek-a-boo. I need to talk to you." Rebecca had always been a precocious child. She said things like "Hi!" and "Mama" within the first four months of her life. By the time she was a year old, she was reciting her full name and phone number to strangers in stores. Now, three years later, her vocabulary is extensive. "Thank you," Rebecca says when he takes his hands down.

Catherine smiles. Rebecca sounds like she does when she needs to speak seriously to her kids. "Charlotte is my favorite doll. That means she is very special to me." Adam nods silently. He doesn't speak much, but his level of understanding has always surprised Catherine.

She fastens the diaper and easily pictures her son attentively listening and nodding. She knows he feels the same way about his truck with the loud horn. He rides it up and down the hallway every chance he gets, but especially loves it when Rebecca pushes him on it.

"We share all of our toys, but Mommy says that we don't have to share one or two that are very special to us. "Rebecca holds up her fingers as she counts it out for him. "I don't want you to touch Charlotte. Ok?"

She waits for Adam to nod again before speaking. "And it's ok to play with my other Barbies because I like when we have pretend parties with them, but their clothes have to stay on. Do you understand?" Her words are mature, and she barely lisps or mispronounces words like other kids her age.

Adam always sighs loudly when he hugs his big sister. "Otay Becky."

Catherine feels a twinge of envy. At just fifteen months old, leaving his sister's favorite doll alone is the most important task of the day.

When Adam releases Rebecca, he runs unsteadily down the hallway. Catherine can hear his diaper

squishing noisily between his legs. "Uh ya ya ya!" he
yells. His voice vibrates with every step he takes. She
stands in the doorway. Maya is cleaned up and fast
asleep on her shoulder. She watches Adam run past her
and stop outside of his own room. "Come, Becky!" he
yells. "Truck!" He makes a sharp left and disappears.

Rebecca drops Charlotte on the couch and hurries
while calling out to him. "Adam! Don't go yet! I'll
push you!"

Catherine smiles. She kisses the top of her baby's
head, grateful that her kids are unique and unusually
sweet, all too aware of what their life could look like if
she let things go.

For that first month, the living room doubles as a
communal bedroom, and the pockets of freshly lit
cigarette smells that Catherine walks into are explained
away as residual and possibly permanent—especially
after she enlists her aunt and mother to help wash
down the filmy yellow windows and bleach the walls.

Soon though, the house is sanitized, and
Catherine liquidates more of her investment portfolio
to buy beds—she worked three jobs and slept two
hours a night for most of her pregnancy just to save
enough to buy the house. She refused to cram herself
and her children into a tiny basement apartment.

Oblivious about how much she has sacrificed for
her family, Adam does not want to sleep in his new big
boy bed. He makes his point almost every night, by
climbing out and crying while wandering through the
house. Determined to train him properly, Catherine
gets up with him. She stumbles around in an exhausted
stupor, to collect and return him to his room.

"Adam, please stay in your bed. If you keep climbing out, I'm going to keep putting you in until you get so tired that you fall asleep here. We might as well just do it right from the beginning."

Adam's lower lip puffs out, his tears threatening to reveal themselves again. Catherine strokes his wet, red cheek. Almost instantly, his eyelids begin to droop. "I know you're mad at me Mister Guy, but I love you."

She kisses his cheek softly. "Can we be friends again?"

Adam nods. She wishes she could forgive as easily as he always does. "How much does Mama love you, baby?" Catherine asks.

"So much, Mama." His little arms extend wide for just a moment before falling heavily to the mattress.

"That's right, my love. I don't want you to ever forget that." After one more kiss, she leaves him and collapses into her own bed. She snuggles up to her soft pillows and drifts off, smiling.

Three weeks, and one nightlight later, it seems as if Adam has given up the fight and Catherine gets more rest, only waking occasionally to nurse Maya, who sleeps peacefully in a crib next to her.

The family settles into their new home, proud of what they have, and seemingly happy. All is well, and Catherine plans to go back to work a month before Christmas, knowing she needs to prepare for the holidays in her new home.

*****

*Every time they give you the medication, her face fades a little bit more. Get it off your tongue. Spit it all out.*

Jeanne is in Florida with her family. She is declining quickly, unencumbered by guilt about how she left her house. About how Catherine has to clean up after her and Manny.

But she's left New York without her beloved doll. When she remembers, she is distraught, and her health worsens. She becomes disoriented and cries out for Anna Maria. Once a day she orders her cousins to search the small condo.

*If you close your eyes, she'll be here. She's always been here, waiting for you to see her. To keep your promise.*

Finally, two months after she arrives in the Sunshine State, Jeanne dies alone in bed, her eyes wide open. Raymond finds her—the cousin that everyone calls Castro because of his resemblance to the Cuban dictator. She is smiling, and her arms are crossed, as if cradling a baby.

Castro prays before leaning over to gently close her eyes. "Sweet dreams Cousin Jeanne. Rest in peace."

His fingertips have not yet touched her translucent eyelids when he stops to study her face. He retracts quickly and wipes his hands on his jeans. When he bends forward again, he's careful not to use the bed or the corpse for support. "What the...??" Castro mutters.

Jeanne's eyes are not the same color blue that they've always been. Instead, the pupils are faded, and the whites of her eyes have disappeared, replaced by glassy, black marbles.

As if he might catch something, Castro grabs a tissue from the bedside—the same ones that the nurses wiped the drool with when Jeanne went on her rants. When she would cry out for her doll. "Anna Maria! Where are you? Oh, how I need you my sweet friend! Please come! Let's finally get rid of Manny!"

Castro uses the tissue to close her eyes. "No offense Cuz, but no one should have to see you like this. Your hair looks burnt and shredded. It's just creepy."

He shudders. Her translucent, pasty skin and the unnatural red of her painted-on lips add to it, making her look like a demon Barbie. An icy finger strokes his spine and he rushes to cover her up with the bed sheet. The next day, Castro is on a plane to Denmark, his intention to miss Jeanne's funeral.

# Chapter 3

*Where am I? What is happening?* Jeanne's head floats weightlessly. *Did I just wake up, or did I black out for a second?*

She moves slowly, carefully avoiding the unfamiliar shapes in front of her and in her peripheral vision. *How did I get out of my room?* She wants to call out, but the heavy silence makes it feel like it would be the wrong thing to do.

There is something in front of her, at her feet. She doesn't have time to step away, so she squinches her eyes and braces herself for pain. But none comes, and Jeanne looks back at where she was. *A Lego?* She keeps moving, feeling almost pulled along. *The layout of this place seems familiar, but something's off.*

Manny's room should be just off the kitchen, but it's not there. Instead, Jeanne finds herself drifting down a long, wide hallway. She knows that's where she wants to be. It's where the answers to all her questions are. *Wait. What? Oh. I know what this is. I'm having a dream. I'll wake up soon.*

A small shaft of light coming from a room on the left tugs at her. Instinctually. she heads for it, feeling more like a passenger and not the driver of this dream.

*Someone is coming.* She doesn't see a shadow, but she can feel a presence. *Just like how I always knew Manny was awake. Right before he'd come into the kitchen and ruin my morning chats with Anna Maria.*

A short figure appears. A small, older woman, in a housecoat. She is far from intimidating, but she scowls and blocks the way into the room. Jeanne stops a few feet from her.

"Where am I?" The woman holds a finger to her lips as if telling Jeanne to be quiet. She is still frowning when she looks across the hall. Jeanne's right arm tingles, and she turns her head to see what has this woman's attention.

She sees a man whose form takes up most of the opening of another room. He glares at her. His arms are folded across his chest. He is wearing a pale yellow, short sleeved, button down shirt—like what guys wore in the early sixties in suburban America. His glasses have thick, plastic frames and his hair is dark and slicked straight back.

"What is going on?" Jeanne asks, looking from one to the other for an answer.

*Don't come any closer.* Jeanne hears the command clearly, but with her mind, not her ears. She can't tell where it came from. *Did they both say it?*

The house is dark except for the pale, faint glow coming from the room behind the tiny woman. Jeanne turns back to the man and peeks past his shoulder. *How am I able to see everything so clearly? Maybe my eyes have adjusted to the dark.*

The bed is backed up against windows, a lump of pillows and blankets unsuccessfully hiding a sleeping form. There are two small dressers, and several art pieces speckle the walls, bringing the room together. It isn't until Jeanne sees the fuse box across from the bed that she discovers where her dreams have taken her.

Because of Manny's paralysis, the fuse box had to be placed on the main floor instead of hidden in the basement. That way, if there was a power outage or an emergency, he could get to it. She realizes that she's in her old New York house just as the body under the blankets snores loudly and flips over.

She steps back, her eyes wide. The man's presence seems to have grown. She can't see past him anymore as he takes over the entire doorway.

A voice echoes angrily in her mind. *What do you want?* This time Jeanne knows it is the woman. She too has become larger and more menacing.

"I don't want anything," Jeanne says. "I don't even know how I got here."

The woman exchanges a look with the man. Jeanne wonders, *Are they going to hurt me?*

*Don't give us a reason to.* The man issues the warning. His mouth hasn't moved, but each word is soaked with hostility.

Jeanne positions herself so that she has eyes on both of them. *How did he know what I was thinking?* She shakes her head to erase it all. *Get a hold of yourself, Jeanne. This is just a dream.*

She looks toward the woman, the older of the two. She was probably once five feet tall, but age has hunched her over. The room she guards is lit by a nightlight. Jeanne can see that a small boy has kicked the covers off, revealing his Winnie the Pooh pajamas.

She stares, her mind clearing. As her illness dissolves, its hold on her finally lifts and she is freed from the cloudy existence she had endured for so many years. *The sewing room... Anna Maria...*she remembers and takes an excited step toward the nightlight, as if that is where her spiritual salvation lies.

The man and woman flank her. The shift is sudden, faster than she's ever seen anyone move. *Are these two even human?* Jeanne is trapped in an electrified embrace, unable to save herself or get to Anna Maria.

*What do you want?* They both ask in unison. The pressure increases when she squirms or tries to fight her way out of it. *Look at it,* the man says without moving his mouth. He nods at her chest with his head.

At first, Jeanne ignores him defiantly. When nothing changes, she reluctantly gives in and looks down at her torso. Wispy, sluggish swirls of dark color swim in and out of her chest. Black, grey, and brown streaks, scarred by angry dashes of red, shoot from her stomach, blazing violently in multiple directions, before being sucked back into her like a vacuum.

Jeanne is momentarily hypnotized. The swampy mix shifts and changes with great effort. She finally tears her eyes away, seeking answers from her captors, whose own colors now circulate in the air around them, much more awake and alive than Jeanne's.

*Where did all of this come from?* What she sees is as confusing as the idea that the man and woman are able to communicate without using their mouths to speak. Jeanne studies them, sorting out who belongs with which colors.

Green, yellow, and light blue waves drift calmly around the old woman, their brightness outlined in silver. They appear orderly, organized, only interrupted by powerful pellets of grey that seize up when they get close to Jeanne.

Indigo, red, and white beams assert the man's power over her. They almost converge with the woman's before turning away to take their own path in and out of his throat and solar plexus. Large brown spots swell from each band, as threatening as the looks they are both giving her.

They move in tandem, combining to trap her and hold her still. Jeanne's colors stop short long before reaching theirs, as if someone has placed a force field at the edge of their boundaries, to block her from joining their alliance.

*What is this?* she wonders, wishing she would wake up. *This dream sucks. The last thing I remember before coming here was Anna Maria calling to me so I could save her from the hole in the wall. I thought I was able to reach her. That I could hold her again.*

The man and the woman exchange knowing looks. They keep her still, but their angry colors calm down until they are merely pockmarks in a sea of tranquility.

It is the man who addresses Jeanne. *You think this is a dream?* he asks.

The older woman leans forward as if she has something to add, but the man puts up a hand. Jeanne thinks he might be stifling a smile.

"Of course this is a dream!" She deliberately excludes herself now, using her mouth to speak even though they can hear her thoughts. "What else would it be? Ya know, you remind me of my stupid husband. You're both dumb as rocks and useless as all hell."

The older woman raises her eyebrows. "What's your story, sister?" Jeanne asks her. "Are you The

Ghost of Christmas Past or something? Did you and the Grim Reaper here team up? To mend my ways so I can go to Heaven when I die?"

The woman smirks. The man pulls a cigarette from a pack in his breast pocket and makes a fist with his thumb tucked under his first two fingers. He flicks his thumb quickly, and like a lighter, a small orangey-blue flame appears at the tip of his nail. Thin streams of whitish-grey smoke mix into his aura, blending in as if it belonged there in the first place.

He takes a long inhale, clearly savoring its taste. Jeanne leans in, hoping to catch a whiff for herself. "So? Where to first? Should we go to my mother's grave, so I can spit on it? Or maybe to where my sons are getting high? You two are the slowest tour guides ever. If I could get a refund, I would."

The man pulls another cigarette from his pack and offers it to her. Jeanne's mother used to call them cancer sticks, but she should've called them her best friends. They were there for Vivien when she was stressed, and they were there when she needed help disciplining the kids. Jeanne looks at her hands. Even now, she has the scars to prove it.

Vivien was so openly infatuated with smoking that it was only natural that Jeanne gave into her own curiosity as a teen. Once she was hooked, she finally understood how her mother coped with a paranoid schizophrenic of a husband and the three kids she didn't bother to raise. Jeanne often marveled at how cigarettes and a shitty home life finally bonded them long after her mother was gone.

Jeanne stares at the man's offering suspiciously.

She only reaches out after she surmises that anything he does to her, any trickery at all, will be erased when she wakes up. *There's nothing he can do here that will permanently scar you.* She grabs the cigarette quickly, in case he plans on snatching it back and sharing a laugh with the old woman, who is watching intently.

The man has given her a Marlboro. Parliaments are her cigarette of choice, but she thinks, *beggars can't be choosers.* Once she has it, she clutches it tightly, never wondering how she's going to light it, instead reveling in the fact that she somehow won a prize. She's managed to invade his space; the angry dots of color didn't keep her back.

The man does that thing with his thumb again and offers her a small flame with which to light up. When she unrolls her fist, she is surprised to see that she is holding a longer, skinnier Parliament.

*Holy shit,* she thinks. *Ooh I get it, I'm starting to control this dream now. Good. It's about time.* As she inhales, the sweet smoke centers her, and she forgets that the man and woman can hear her thoughts. *The next thing I'm going to do is get these two idiots out of my way. I want to hold Anna Maria before I wake up.*

Neither one makes an effort to hide their amusement.

*What is so funny?* Jeanne thinks as they laugh at her. The sound is loud but hollow, and this time their mouths are open. *It's about time,* Jeanne thinks, *I'm so sick of that I'm so creepy, I never move my lips shit.*

As if catching themselves, both the man and woman purse their lips into tight, thin lines and the laughing stops.

*I'm Richard, and this is Elizabeth.* The man introduces them.

*Who are you?* Elizabeth asks.

"I'm Jeanne," she says with her mouth. "If you guys can just let me see my doll, then I'll finally wake up and be out of your way. Or if you're supposed to take me somewhere, just let me get my doll and I'll go wherever you want. This standoff we've got going on here is annoying, to be honest."

*I'm just going to tell her. She's actually more annoying than this standoff is, if you ask me,* Richard says.

Elizabeth answers him, *Yeah, tell her, but take it easy. You are so close. Don't mess it up by getting sucked into her low vibration. You have a lot at stake here.*

Richard looks behind him, back into the room he has been blocking. Then he takes a thoughtful drag on his cigarette before addressing Jeanne. *Ok, here it is. You're not in a dream. You're not going to wake up. In fact, you're not going anywhere because you're dead.* His statements seem suspended in midair for a moment before the full impact comes crashing down.

Jeanne points a finger at him. "Ya know what? This is bullshit and I'm done!" She looks up at the ceiling in the hallway. The light fixtures are different. And the new owners have installed an extra one right above where she stands. "I wanna wake up now!"

Jeanne puts the cigarette in her mouth while she pinches herself and shakes her body. Ashes fall from the burnt edge, dissolving into nothing before they hit the floor.

She doesn't feel the pinch. Instead, her fingers squeeze the swirling colors around her arm. They flare up, sparking and startling her into quickly letting go. She yells, and she tries to jump up and down, but she can't get her feet to touch the floor.

Elizabeth and Richard watch her silently. She searches their faces for answers before she realizes that they too are floating about six inches above the hardwood floor. The outline of their shoes is barely visible.

Jeanne runs for the front door, but her hand floats right through the knob when she grabs for it. Pain, like the sting of a hundred angry bees, radiates up her arm. Violent sparks burst into the air, as if her arm is robotic and about to explode.

When she recovers from the initial shock and discomfort, she turns and races into the living room. Richard and Elizabeth are already there when she arrives, smiling and waving at her mockingly from the other side of the coffee table.

"No! That's not true! I am not dead! This is a dream!" She squinches her eyes shut and whines.

Elizabeth sighs. *Let's just leave her for now. She'll figure it out.*

*I am so sick of her. She's in our space. And what does a grown woman want with a doll? It's a trick. She knows she's dead. She wants to hurt the kids,* Richard complains. The colors around him darken and dim.

Jeanne slowly opens her eyes, hoping that she'll be back in bed, but instead she finds herself still in the old house, watching an exchange between two strangers.

Elizabeth reaches out to Richard. *Be careful. You don't want to backslide,* Elizabeth says.

He nods and drops his cigarette. It disappears, but he stamps it out as if both he and it are still Earth bound. His pool of colors slows down enough to let some indigo and white creep back in. He squares himself with Jeanne. *Don't you think you should've woken up by now? Isn't this the longest dream you've ever had?* Even his thoughts sound sarcastic.

Suddenly, Jeanne's back tingles. She knows that someone is behind her in the hallway and spins around to see the profile of a child in the blackness.

*She's sleepwalking again,* Richard and Elizabeth say in unison.

In less time than it would take Jeanne to walk there, they appear next to the dark shadow. Elizabeth uses her colorful energy to steer the young girl in the direction of the bathroom Jeanne had passed earlier. Richard looks on as if supervising.

Jeanne crumples to a spot just above the floor. Her so called body rests heavily in the air as she tries to make sense of what is going on. *Boy, I could use another cigarette,* she thinks, and a pack of Parliaments appears in her hand.

She puts one in her mouth and tries unsuccessfully to light it using her thumb like Richard did. Jeanne sighs and stares at her finger. *Well, if nothing else, I can taste the tobacco.* As quickly as she has the thought, a small flame appears at the tip of her thumbnail.

## Chapter 4

In dead time, hours, minutes, and days pass as if they are mere seconds, and sleep is no longer a necessity. Jeanne cannot leave the house, so she skulks in corners, avoiding Richard and Elizabeth.

The family who lives there now goes about their daily routines without acknowledging any of them. The children jump out of bed in the morning and whisper sleepy goodnights to the moon several times before Jeanne finally realizes that she is not going to wake up. That she really is dead.

When she gasps loudly, Richard and Elizabeth freeze. The looks they give her could probably kill her a second time. Catherine and the kids lift their faces from their breakfast bowls, cocking their heads and listening.

"Mama, did you hear that?" The child who had been sleepwalking asks the question. Jeanne now knows her as Rebecca, the oldest.

Catherine answers, "Yeah, I think it was just a bird. They make all kinds of crazy noises."

Jeanne wonders just how many gasps from the dead can be heard. These gasps of revelation, of acceptance, the marking of this rite of passage from one realm to the next. The intake of a useless breath of air, signifying that death has begun for another soul. She hypothesizes that they are heard as often as the cries of newborn babies, celebrating the contrary— their entry into the world with hearts that beat to the rhythm of the living.

*I can't believe I'm a fucking ghost!* Jeanne clamps

a hand over her mouth as if she said it out loud. As if God might hear her thoughts and keep her from the Pearly Gates because of her bad language.

*I'd better clean that up before I go toward the light. Speaking of which...* She searches up and down, right and left, behind and in front of herself. There is no evidence of a "light". It isn't following her, ready to scoop her up. *Great. Another urban myth.*

Still, she refrains from cursing again. *Just in case. This can't be all there is. If it was, there'd be more people...and they'd be a hellava lot more interesting than these two...*

She is being pushed along, without a say in what happens next. Her personality is intact—Jeanne's soul carries with it the lessons and perspectives she gathered in life.

Knowing that her body is dead, but her mind is still conscious sinks in, and she's suddenly eager to get this phase over with and move on to a better place.

*Everything feels the same though.* Her hands have the same veiny, spindly fingers they always did, and they still ache to wrap themselves around Manny's neck and choke him.

*There's no forgiveness in the afterlife*, she muses, and smiles at the thought of haunting him. *I could follow his fat ass around and poke him all day long.*

The thought pulls at her. Suddenly afraid that she might wind up with him instead of in the house where Anna Maria is, Jeanne reconsiders. *Forget that. He's got some nasty habits I won't miss and why would I even want to spend any more time with him? I'm finally free!*

Months fly by. The house takes on a newer, happier vibe as thick coats of laughter and love are laid down within the bones of their home. Almost all traces of Manny, her sons, and their dysfunction disappear. If not for some stray pieces of junk mail still being delivered, the Parnicellos would be completely forgotten.

Richard's constant presence keeps Jeanne on edge. He smokes his Marlboros and watches her like a sentry. When electric prickles temporarily paralyze her, she knows that she's come too close to the kids for his liking. He's their guard dog, and if Jeanne ever heard him growl, she wouldn't be surprised.

On the flip side, she watches him use his energy to push toys out from under the couches so the kids can find their dolls and building blocks. He smiles when they play at his feet.

Elizabeth comes and goes, mostly at night, when she attaches herself to Catherine and the baby. If she is there during the day, Elizabeth helps around the house. Except for a few deliberate moments, she often goes unnoticed.

The basement will remain unfinished for a few more years, and although the kids are not allowed to go down there, that is where Catherine does laundry. Jeanne follows along, looking for anything to entertain herself. Elizabeth is not far behind.

Catherine doesn't have a laundry basket, so she pulls as much clean stuff from the dryer as she can hold. Unfortunately, one washcloth falls to the floor. She stops short, frantically looking from the pile she's holding to the lone piece of fabric lying helplessly at her feet.

Jeanne almost laughs out loud. *I used to know people like this. If she doesn't pick that up right away, she's gonna want to burn it rather than use it.*

Picking up one small washcloth with so many towels in her arms will cause more to fall. Elizabeth and Jeanne both smile when Catherine takes a deep breath and leaves it where it is.

Jeanne shadows her upstairs. She watches Catherine put the laundry down on the couch, then step outside to bring in the trash cans the garbagemen have left scattered at the curb. Manny's handicap ramp is gone, replaced by stones and flowers that bring new life to Jeanne's old home.

She keeps her hands and face from touching the glass on the front door. She learned the hard way that the door is a painful barrier that keeps her in no matter how many times she tries to run right through it. Jeanne stands close, imagining that she can feel the breeze.

Catherine walks past her when she comes inside and returns to the basement to pick up the washcloth. But she stops short, her mouth a perfectly round *O* when she gasps. The washcloth sits on top of a small drying rack, neatly spread out as if it had been there all night, waiting to be folded with the rest of the laundry. Catherine takes a couple of hesitant steps toward the rack.

Elizabeth leans against one of the metal poles that help support the ceiling and smiles. *Oh, give me a break, you smug bitch. What's the big deal?* Jeanne's eyes dart from the washcloth to the stairs. *Richard is watching the kids play in Rebecca's room. He won't come.*

Elizabeth ignores her.

*I'm going to make it dance,* Jeanne thinks. *That oughta scare the crap outta her.* She smirks at Elizabeth, unaware that with her hair in patches on her wrinkled scalp and her pasty complexion, her expression resembles the Joker's grimace.

Her long, determined strides carry her quickly. She throws down her lit cigarette and it dissolves into thin air before hitting the floor. Fueled by ego, Jeanne reaches over to snatch up the washcloth, but her hand passes through the fabric and the thin wood of the rack. She comes out the other side holding nothing but air.

It doesn't hurt, but there is a shift in energy when she hits the mass. Her dark, angry colors move out of the way, making room for blues and greens created by the natural materials found in the cotton and the wood.

After Catherine catches her breath, she inches slowly toward the drying rack, eyeing the washcloth suspiciously. When she scoops it up, her hand passes right through Jeanne's arm. Jeanne feels familiar electric tingles. Then, her arm drops to her side like dead weight.

Catherine shivers and hugs herself. "Thank you," she says to the empty space around her, before she heads back to the stairs.

"Why can't I pick things up like you can?" Jeanne asks Elizabeth, using her mouth instead of her thoughts.

The rubber on the bottom of Catherine's sneaker squeaks when she stops short. She turns back toward the washer and dryer, searching as if something or somebody is there, but she can't quite make them out. Elizabeth smiles, then disappears instead of answering Jeanne.

Her stomach pushes out an angry black bubble. *Am I ever going to see Anna Maria again, or am I just stuck here with these weirdos and those brats forever?*

She heads for the steps and flings an arm forward as if to push Catherine out of her way. Jeanne's murky colors briefly invade Catherine's space, but they are swallowed up by her joyful, pastel aura. Its natural state of positivity weakens Jeanne and she falls over, onto her side.

She struggles to stand. She searches the colors that surround Catherine, frowning when she realizes that her dark smudges haven't imprinted on the woman's spirit. Like a dunce cap, she wears a muddied blue cone of disappointment above her head and follows Catherine upstairs.

\*\*\*\*\*

Jeanne stews while she watches Elizabeth and Richard hover over the kids. *Look at those stalkers grinning. What are they? Sickos or something?! Is this all it's ever going to be for me?*

When she sees Elizabeth with the new baby, she's usually standing next to the crib across from Catherine's bed. Jeanne creeps close to peek—*it may not be TV, but it's better than looking at walls, full of pictures of people and places I don't care about.*

Suddenly, Richard materializes, a silvery grey, protective shield swirling bigger and darker each time Jeanne considers challenging him.

Finally, one night, she pleads her case. "Can you guys cut me a break here?"

Elizabeth lifts her hand out of the crib and puts a finger to her lips. *We can hear you just fine if you just think what you want to say. Maya wakes up because of your voice.*

Jeanne nods and agrees. Maybe if she compromises, they'll help her. She clenches her fists and juts her neck forward as if she's directing the stream of thoughts. *There. I'm not using my mouth. Now will you guys please talk to me and answer some of my questions? As much as I want to, I'm obviously not leaving anytime soon.*

Richard defers to Elizabeth. She looks back on Maya and Catherine then makes a shooing motion with her hands, ordering Richard and Jeanne away from the bedroom, down the hallway, and into the living room.

*What do you want to know?* Elizabeth asks.

They stand in a small circle around the coffee table, eyeing each other suspiciously.

*How do you guys do what you do? All of it.* Jeanne knows that anything she learns might help her reunite with Anna Maria.

Richard shakes his head no and folds his arms across his chest. He stares at Elizabeth intently.

At first, Jeanne is confused. Elizabeth's thoughts seem random. *Richard don't be like that. Try and understand. What if I had treated you badly based on your aura?*

When she realizes that she can't hear Richard's responses, Jeanne covers her mouth to keep from speaking out loud. *Holy crap! You can block your thoughts too?*

*Yes, we can.* Elizabeth answers plainly. *I wish you'd do the same with your curse words. There's no reason for such talk here.*

If Jeanne were still alive, the skin on her face would flame a shameful red. Instead, her eyes reveal her when they release pinwheels of black embarrassment. She drops her head, defeated.

Elizabeth nudges Richard with a milky elbow and he lightens up. *Sorry Jeanne. I know how it feels. Before Elizabeth showed up, I was confused and lonely too.*

Their compassion is surprising enough to erase Jeanne's shame with an audible whoosh. Elizabeth and Richard's dark splotches settle down, circling her cautiously instead of jumping at her.

Jeanne looks at her legs. A pale, buttercup yellow ribbon is slowly winding its way up her body, carefully navigating around puddles of greys and blacks.

*That's hope,* Elizabeth offers.

Her hate and anger temporarily sidelined, Jeanne sits cross-legged in the air, relaxing for the first time since she arrived. She lights a cigarette and Richard does the same, taking a seat a few inches above the long couch. A beer can appears, and he opens it, his cigarette dangling from his lips, so he can use both hands.

Elizabeth remains standing, smoothing the wrinkles in her housecoat before pulling a wadded up tissue from her pocket and fiddling with it.

*Her hands are always busy,* Jeanne thinks.

Elizabeth replies, *Idle hands are the devil's workplace.*

This strikes both Richard and Elizabeth as funny, but for once, Jeanne doesn't feel left out. She dives in with questions. *What's your story? How do you guys know each other? Are you just two dead people who happened to meet? It can't be the house that brought you here because my husband and I were the ones that had it built.*

Richard points at a large crack snaking its way up one of the supporting walls. *Yeah, nice job,* he says.

Jeanne shrugs. *We got a lot of grants because of Manny's time in the military and his injuries. He cheaped out on the house so he could keep a bunch of the money to buy pot.* She takes a drag on her cigarette and nods toward the hallway. *I think I'm here for my doll. What about you two?*

Richard winks at Elizabeth. *You explain it Betty. It's way too complicated for me to tell it right.*

*We're here for them.* Elizabeth points to where Catherine and her children are sleeping. *Catherine is my granddaughter and the babies are my great-grandchildren.* A bright blue flame engulfs Elizabeth, temporarily shrouding her in its intensity.

Jeanne pulls back, but Richard reassures her. *That's love. And nobody loves like Betty does.*

Richard and Elizabeth shoot sapphire arrows at each other to drive their point home. They intertwine, as if to hug first before each show of affection returns to its owner.

*Why won't the colors around me come near yours?* Jeanne asks.

Elizabeth explains, *Those colors are your aura—the energies that you put out. In your case, the blacks and greys around you suck in light and energy.* She nods at Jeanne. *You are vibrating so low that if we were to interact more closely with you, you could drag us down to your level and it would be hard to work our way back up.*

She smiles and points at the ceiling. *We choose to stay close to the Source—what you call God. We keep you away from Catherine and the kids because your low vibration could hurt them. Are you following so far?* Elizabeth sips from the steamy coffee mug that has suddenly appeared in her hand. The tissue is back in her pocket, and she remains standing on thick, stockinged legs.

Jeanne nods, eyes wide. *Ok. I get why you don't want me around those guys, but what's your deal?* She is looking at Richard.

He sighs before he starts. *Betty is my mother-in-law...actually, ex-mother-in-law...and Catherine is my daughter. The kids are my grandchildren.* He lowers his face, but his aura gives him away. A dull blue appears at its edge, threatening to creep in and drown out all of the happy colors.

Jeanne leans in eagerly. *I love gossip.*

Elizabeth shoots black dagger warnings at Jeanne before turning to Richard.

*I can't...*Richard wilts. A gloomy brown seeps into his mix, warping and bending its former brightness with his insecurities.

*No, Richard. Don't do this. Look at me.* Elizabeth gets close to him. She burns a fluorescent blue once more, reminding Jeanne of her former life. When stained glass images of the Blessed Mother kneeling next to her son's crumpled body inspired her to pray for better days.

*I love you. You know I do. I will not give up on you. We are in this together, so stay focused. There is so much more for you on the other side. I promise.* Elizabeth's hand glows a radiant white as she strokes him, easing out the murkiness and helping him to return to his calm, natural state.

*What's happening?* Jeanne asks.

*Richard did not always make the best decisions in life,* Elizabeth says.

The two lock eyes, but Richard shakes his head. *It's just too hard*, he says.

Elizabeth tells his story for him. *Richard was an adult when he found out that his mother had left him to be raised by his grandparents. He loved them and they loved him, but all along he had known that something was off. He had never felt good enough and got into the habit of drinking away his difficulties.*

Elizabeth narrates without breaks, as if relaying it quickly will minimize the pain.

*He got married and had Catherine, but he was never truly happy. And neither were his wife and daughter. They grew used to living without him and he created a world that didn't include them.*

*He took frequent trips home to see his family, who saw him as fun loving. Laughing at his jokes was easy. They enjoyed the man who did not spend his time passed out on the living room couch, an empty six pack on the floor beside him. They enjoyed the guy who didn't yell or curse or threaten them.*

*Right or wrong, for a long time, Solo Richard had a better life than Married Dad Richard did. That guy had a girlfriend who didn't expect to be supported. She didn't question his whereabouts. He could come and go as he pleased, with no bills to pay or kids to be responsible for.*

Her blue and white lights snake through Richard's aura, popping any browns or blacks it comes upon. He tilts his head toward Elizabeth and lets his colors reach out to hers for more comfort.

*Eventually, my daughter got fed up and threw him out of the house he rarely slept in anyway. Some years before, his kidney had failed. By then, his body was rejecting the first transplant and a second one would be necessary. His work was suffering, and his health was failing.*

Jeanne catches herself wishing she had been like Richard's wife, that she had left Manny to fend for himself, so she could have had a happier life.

Elizabeth continues, *His world began crashing down, so he moved in with his girlfriend. Things got worse and he got even sicker—with cancer—but that's not what killed him.*

Jeanne absentmindedly lights another cigarette, still leaning forward, now an attentive and respectful audience.

*Many would say that before his illnesses could do him in, Karma had a go at him first. Caring for and financially supporting a man she had never really intended to be so committed to became too much. His girlfriend asked him to move out.* Elizabeth stops the story there. She looks to Richard for permission to go on. When he nods, black spots of his own shame wink at Jeanne as if they share a secret.

Again, Elizabeth sends her energy in while she speaks. Like a search and destroy mission, those black spots explode until they bleed and blend into his usual greens. *At the end of his life, Richard chose to commit suicide. He escaped his pain without making things right with the people he left behind.*

Elizabeth sips from her coffee mug. *Except he didn't escape anything at all. As soon as he left his body, he thought of his daughter. His regret carried him right to her, chaining him to the idea that he cannot and should not move on. He has been with her ever since, doing what he can to act as a father figure, protecting her, her kids, and showing them that he is here.*

*Wait a second,* Jeanne says, *What do you mean, "showing them that he is here"?*

At the mention of the duty he has sworn to carry out, subtle blue sparks bounce off of Richard. This time he is the one to explain. *Children come here fresh and ready to experience everything they can. They don't know fear, embarrassment, or hate until they are taught it. They don't shut us out until someone shows them how to be afraid of death. Or until someone explains the uncertainty of what waits for them beyond the life they have just begun.*

*So, these kids can see us?* Jeanne asks.

Elizabeth answers, *Usually, they are too*

*preoccupied with absorbing everything around them. This is a new space and it's exciting for them, so after a while, they forget about where they came from, only focusing on what they came here to do—learn life lessons and to experience new perspectives. But once in a while, the intoxication with "what is" lifts and they can see us.*

Jeanne studies the rows and rows of books that line the walls. She has seen Catherine read each night before bed. *I never realized how big this room was when I lived here. I wonder if I learned anything while I was alive.*

Richard lights another cigarette and finishes his beer. After a long draw, he explains further, blowing out puffs of smoke with every word. *For example, Rebecca, the oldest, is a really smart kid who started talking very early. One day, when she was only eleven months old, I stood behind my daughter and waved to the baby while she was on the changing table. I wasn't sure she would see me, but Rebecca smiled and waved back. Catherine turned around, but she couldn't see me.*

*She asked Rebecca, "Who are you waving to?"*
*And Rebecca answered, "The man."*

*While Catherine put a fresh diaper on her, she asked questions about what I looked like. Rebecca described me well enough for Catherine to tell her, "I think your Grandpa Richie is here, saying hi to you."* Richard's love for them shines brightly.

Jeanne cocks her head and waves an impatient finger at both of them. She doesn't want to hear any more stories about people and events that have nothing to do with her. *Show me how to move things.*

Elizabeth nods at Jeanne's aura. It lightens up a bit as the grey and black bits reluctantly move to make way for the yellow band of hope that is still there. It spreads eagerly when she imagines being reunited with Anna Maria.

*Alright,* Richard says, *The first thing you need to do is relax. If you're desperate or coming from a bad place, it's just not gonna happen. And don't fake it. Your feelings have to be for real because Source knows. Source knows more than we know about ourselves.*

*What the hell does that even mean?* Jeanne thinks.

The other two smile. *It's sort of confusing and a little bit overwhelming, but once you get into it, the whole thing makes sense.*

Elizabeth's encouragement coaxes out tiny blue dots in Jeanne's aura. When she succumbs to Elizabeth's soothing tone, pale yellow stripes begin to deepen in color around her hands. They tingle with an eagerness to perform.

*What's happening?* With her palms open and in the air, Jeanne looks like she is surrendering.

*Don't lose it,* Richard says.

Elizabeth helps, *Everything is fine. Nothing bad is happening.* She allows one small wave of energy to comingle with the bright buttercup yellow in Jeanne's hands. She caresses it with her own golden glow.

After the lecture she got earlier, Jeanne is surprised that Elizabeth would take such liberties with her life force. Soon, Jeanne's hands look like chubby ducklings, the kind that mothers use to line their kids' Easter baskets with.

Elizabeth says, *She's all set, Richard. Start small.*

For the first time in a long time, Jeanne waits patiently for instructions, happy to go with the flow.

The kids have left a sippy cup on the living room table. Richard reaches toward it and pushes it in Jeanne's direction. His finger extends, but it is the violet energy shooting from it that wraps itself around the cup and urges it forward. *It's all about intention. Where do you want it to go? Just think about what you want and point.*

Jeanne reaches out her own finger. A silver outline has joined the yellow energy and she flicks it as if dismissing an underling. Her colors muddy quickly, and the cup stays where it is.

"Aww, come on!" Jeanne shouts.

Elizabeth looks back over her shoulder, toward the bedrooms. Jeanne clamps a hand over her mouth. *Sorry. I forgot.*

*You're not quite getting it.* Richard explains, *You not only have to want it to move, but you also need to think of exactly where you want it to go. For now, it will be awkward, and you will have to think of it like ticking off a checklist, but later, the process will come naturally.*

After two cigarettes and four more fails, Jeanne finally moves the sippy cup three inches to the left, in front of Richard. She whoops and Elizabeth shushes her, although she also smiles and claps.

It feels like no time has passed, but suddenly it's dawn and the baby whimpers then cries out to be changed. Elizabeth moves the cup to the sink.

Jeanne watches it float into the next room. *That's amazing.*

*We'll pick this up again after they go to bed tonight,* Elizabeth says, before disappearing from in front of them.

Jeanne turns to Richard, who is relaxing with a Marlboro. *Where does she go when she's not here?*

*She can move in and out of the light as she pleases,* Richard says. *She's always trying to get me to join her.* He sighs. *It's just not that easy.*

When his head turns toward the hallway, Jeanne's eyes follow. She is surprised to see Catherine standing there, holding Maya and staring straight at them.

Jeanne doesn't know what to do, so she looks to Richard for guidance. It is clear that he has forgotten her. He grins, poised as if ready to jump up and hug his family.

Catherine is sniffing the air when Rebecca peeks out from behind her mother. "Mommy, what are you doing?" she asks.

"Hey, baby girl. I smell cigarettes. In fact, I smell the cigarettes that my dad used to smoke."

"Ew!" Rebecca says. "Smoking is bad for you. I don't want to smell that."

Catherine smiles. Her eyes are still on Jeanne and Richard. "I know, but it reminds me of my dad..."

Her voice trails off. Rebecca coos at Maya. "Hello baby sister. I love you so much. Give me a kiss." When Catherine lets Rebecca sit on the couch to hold Maya, Richard inches closer to them.

Jeanne remains standing, shifting her weight

from one foot to the other, folding and unfolding her hands. Even in death, she is an awkward fly on the wall, still not fitting in without Anna Maria by her side.

*****

After many months that feel like mere hours, Jeanne finally gets the hang of moving things around. She practices on progressively larger objects until one night, Richard presents her with the Holy Grail of their tiny paranormal world—the heavy wooden coffee table in the living room. The table that Jeanne heard Catherine say was a housewarming gift from her friend Samantha.

Elizabeth hasn't popped in yet, but the dynamic between Richard and Jeanne has changed enough that a mediator is no longer necessary.

*Ok. This is it. If you can push this thing, you've officially graduated from Ghost Moves 101.* Richard reaches out his hand and extends a green streak that playfully nudges the table toward Jeanne. It groans against the bare floor.

She scrambles backward, still too new to this dimension to remember that physical objects go through her, leaving her unharmed. When she grins, the gaps between her rotted teeth emit little pink orbs that celebrate her accomplishment. *Alright. Here we go. But if I can't move it, it's not me. It means that I had a shitty teacher.*

Jeanne looks for Elizabeth to appear, hands on hips, and scolding her for her bad language. When she doesn't materialize, Jeanne reaches out both hands and bends her knees, posed like a ninja, as if this is a big job.

Her aura is still muddy and dark, but spatters of reds, blues, and violet fade in and out, a dull glitter that sparkles when the light hits it. Her yellow ribbon of hope twists and winds among the gloomier shades, like the road in the Wizard of Oz, leading the way to redemption in the black dark of her soul.

When the table inches toward Richard, she drops her hands as if she's been burned. She uses her mouth when she exclaims, "Holy shit!"

Their eyes lock, and the mischievous devils that they were in life meet each other for their first otherworldly play date. Their energy is lighthearted, snowballing and growing stronger as they fool around with the furniture.

*****

When Elizabeth pops in to check on a fast-asleep Maya, the living room is dense with swirls of bright whites, yellows and reds. They zoom in and around each other so quickly, that trying to tell which colors belong to which soul is impossible.

Elizabeth looks down at her great-grandchild; Maya has already begun walking and climbs out of the crib in the mornings on her own. *This one is spunky, like her mom. She's going to be a handful.*

Her hands glow an iridescent turquoise. They fill with an energy that tingles so intensely it must be released. She reaches down until she is immersed in

Maya's aura. It is thick with blues and whites, tranquil, like a sea that laps gently against the shore. Elizabeth allows herself to be rocked slowly, lost in Maya's spirit.

Suddenly, a series of short, deep, grating sounds tear through her reverie, waking her like an unwelcome alarm clock that rings before dawn. Elizabeth stops stroking Maya's head. She can hear that Richard and Jeanne have forgotten themselves when the table pushes and groans against the floor, and their open mouth laughing echoes eerily throughout the house.

Hand poised above the crib, she listens for a second before rushing down the hallway and into the living room.

*****

The baby is quiet, but Catherine stirs. She swings her legs off the side of the bed and listens.

*What is that noise? It sounds like little feet pattering down the hall. Adam! He's out of bed, but what is he doing? He's going to hurt himself!* Her fear propels her off the mattress and into the hallway.

She peeks into Adam's room. He's fast asleep, clutching Pooh Bear, his nightlight protecting him from the dark.

The scraping of wood on wood tears through her relief. She identifies the sound easily. *The coffee table! Rebecca! She must be sleepwalking again!*

She hurries down the hall. The last time, Rebecca had wandered into the living room, dropped her pants and crouched, prepared to pee all over the easy chair, thinking it was the toilet.

Catherine stops short when she hears her five-year old snoring in her bed. Unarmed, but prepared to beat down the intruder with her slipper, she sneaks forward a few more feet. The racket is loud enough to hurt her ears when she flips on the light in the living room.

The table is exactly where it should be, and no one is there. *I heard the table moving! I'm sure of it!* Doubt shadows her as she checks the kitchen and both bathrooms. They are all empty and the locks on the doors are secure. Even the house alarm is activated, ensuring that no one can enter or leave the house without it going off.

*Did the neighbor's cat sneak in?* She searches under beds and behind dressers but finds nothing.

Heart pounding, she returns to the living room, but she doesn't see Elizabeth, Richard, and Jeanne frozen like statues.

*****

After being reprimanded by Elizabeth, the lessons continue, and Jeanne becomes more proficient at controlling her surroundings. As long as her intentions are good and she has enough energy, she can pick things up, move objects around, and conjure most of what she desires at will.

Richard and Elizabeth are still guarded. She isn't allowed to perform any tricks in front of Catherine and the kids, and they still block the way to her beloved doll. But Jeanne is confident that sooner or later they will ease up and she will see Anna Maria again.

Like it or not, Jeanne has gotten to know the family. Adam is an explorer and, in her opinion, the most interesting of the lot. He has an instinctive need to touch and learn how things work.

Jeanne laughs when he gets his head stuck in the railing on the back deck and his foot caught in the spindles on the kitchen chairs. He stuffs his mouth with an entire half of a peanut butter and jelly sandwich before he chokes on it and has to be rescued by his mother. When Catherine reaches in and pulls out the pile of half eaten bread with her hand, Jeanne frowns. She would never have done that for her boys.

Adam takes apart Rebecca's toy refrigerator, and happily puts it back together when his sister cries about how *he's ruined it*. When he's done, he goes in search of new terrain. He seems to be curious about everything.

Jeanne follows him, hoping that he'll see her. Then she can scare him *since he's so damn nosy all the time.*

"Adam, how did this dresser get over here?" Catherine pushes it back against the wall in his room, covering the square hole she found when she moved in.

Adam is sitting on the floor playing, but he stops and raises his chubby hands. "Me, Mama. I so strong."

Jeanne is standing in the hallway outside Adam's room. She scoffs and Richard appears, his aura outlined in black and jumping at her like an electrified fence. He puts a finger to his lips, but Jeanne ignores him and looks over his shoulder at the scene.

Catherine takes her boy in her arms and lifts him over her head. "Strong like this?"

He squeals and giggles. "Ha, ha! Yes, Mama! Yes! More!"

"Are you sure you want more?"

"Yes!"

"Alright. You asked for it." She grins and spins around, letting his legs fly. Adam screams with joy.

When she places him back down on the floor, she kneels in front of him. "Look at me, baby. You are so strong, but do not move that dresser any more. If it falls on you, you'll get hurt. And if you get hurt, what will I do then?"

"You cry, Mama."

"Exactly. So, if you want to do strong, tough guy things, tell me and I'll give you stuff to move. Ok?" She takes his chin in her hands to distract him from the toy train he has just picked up. "Are you hearing me? Nothing can happen to my boy."

She hugs him as he answers her. "Yes, Mama."

"Now tell me how much I love you."

Adam's spreads his arms wide. "So, so much," he says.

Catherine is halfway down the hall when Adam stands up and heads for a pile of toys in the corner, by his bed. Jeanne gasps when he pulls out a doll from beneath the large building blocks. He sits Anna Maria on one of his trucks.

"Adam? Are you ok, sweetie?" Catherine calls back over her shoulder.

"Yes, Mama," he answers.

Jeanne struggles to get into the room, but Richard

has become a solid grey wall. Like a steel barricade, it keeps Jeanne's swirling mass of black and brown energy from lurching forward, toward Adam.

She paces, the colors around her churn slowly, melting together into a murky swamp of darkness that no sane soul would ever want to fall into.

*I haven't shown you all I can do,* Richard warns. *Stay away from the boy.*

Jeanne's eyes have all but disappeared, replaced instead by sunken black marbles. She bares her teeth at him. They are as fractured and decayed as her chances for transitioning to the other side.

She tries to peek past him one more time, before giving up and moving away. He is glowing, his love casting such a light that there aren't enough shadows for her to hide in.

# Chapter 5

Richard and Elizabeth huddle close, no doubt talking about Jeanne. She stares at the chairs in the kitchen and considers throwing one of them at the pair, *but what's the point? It won't hurt them.* She is shrouded by her own dark aura, the weight of her despair threatening to swallow her up.

In the living room, Catherine and her cousin are sprawled out on the couches, giggling as the TV rambles on in the background.

*They sound like the nonstop chatter I used to hear when I was alive. When it was hard to think straight. Ugh, I really want to squash these two like bugs.* Jeanne sneers at them. She enjoys imagining that when they turn to look in her direction, they can sense that she is there.

*****

Richard and Elizabeth exclude Jeanne from their thoughts.

*Do you see it?* Elizabeth asks. *It's happening.* When she motions down the hallway, excited pink and silver sparks lead the way.

Richard watches Catherine's head follow her grandmother's hand as if she is part of the conversation. A small light glows and pulses in the middle of the front door. It is about the size of a dime, but its brightness makes it appear bigger and stronger.

He frowns and turns his attention on Jeanne. *I can't go yet. Look at her.*

Jeanne floats above one of the kitchen chairs, crouched like a rabid animal and glaring at the girls through blackened sockets. Yellow drool trickles down her chin before disappearing into the air. It is the last of her hope, the last of what good remained, seeping out, desperate to escape the thing she has become.

Richard is startled out of his thoughts when Catherine says, "Hey Sara, I keep getting the strangest feeling that the front door is going to open, and a man...I mean my dad...is going to come in. And I smell wine. Do you smell it? It's so strong."

He looks down at the glass in his hand. Despite Jeanne's drastic transformation, Elizabeth had encouraged Richard to celebrate how close he is to crossing over. But when Jeanne lets out a menacing hiss, he finds it hard to enjoy the merlot that was his favorite when he was alive.

Sara says, "Yeah, I keep looking at it, thinking that somebody is going to walk in too, although I didn't consider that it could be your dad. I'm trying to be cool, but you know this stuff scares me." She glances at the kitchen.

"Why do you keep looking over there?" Catherine asks.

Sara's eyes shift quickly between her cousin and Jeanne. "I don't know", she mumbles.

"I feel like one of those chairs is about to come flying at us," Catherine says.

When Sara nods, Richard interprets it as a confession that she feels it too.

"It seems like an angry energy. And the only person I know who is that angry is my father. Plus, there's the wine smell. He's here. I know it. And he's not happy."

Richard's face falls and the light by the door dims.

*Stop it, Richard.* Elizabeth strokes his energy with hers. *She doesn't understand.*

He keeps his eyes on Jeanne. She lights up a Parliament, sucking on it and letting it burn down to her fingers. Before the ashes fall into nothingness and she's left with only the filter, she deliberately blows smoke at the girls.

Richard lurches forward, but Elizabeth holds him back with one electrified arm, forcing him to watch helplessly.

Jeanne's aura turns thick and gooey when she inches toward Sara. Her form is like a dark, melty gummy worm that has come to life and wants to sit on its victim's lap.

Sara shivers and shrinks into the couch. "I know Cath, I feel it too. It's so heavy."

"Right?" Catherine says. Then she asks, "You know what we have to do?"

"Please. I hate when you talk to them."

"I've heard that when you're scared, ghosts feed off of it and the problem becomes worse. I've got kids here. He needs to calm down."

Richard's sad browns deepen. *That's what she thinks of me? That I'd scare her or hurt the kids? She doesn't know how much I love them all. How sorry I am for how I treated her.*

*Stop it Richard.* Elizabeth chastises him. *Don't lose yourself. Be present so she can see your light and love. Self pity is what ended your mortal life. You want it to destroy your chance at eternal life as well?* Her stern words are reflected in sharp colors that hack into his dull ones, cutting the brown orbs in half, then in quarters.

*Where is your wine?* she asks. *Get it. You've done nothing wrong, and the smell will let her know that you are here, regardless of what that one pulls.* Elizabeth jerks a thumb in Jeanne's direction. She is hunched over, weighed down by a sickly-looking, dark green ball that has attached itself to her back.

Catherine sits up straight at the edge of the loveseat. "Ya know what? I don't like the vibe you're putting out, Dad. Cut it out...or better yet, show me what a tough guy you really are. Throw the chair. Go ahead. I know you want to."

Sara shakes her head before hiding her face in her hands. Her voice is muffled when she speaks. "Why do you have to push it? Just tell him to stop and let's move on."

"Aren't you the least bit curious? Wouldn't it be cool if he could actually do it?" Catherine's aura, although invisible to her and Sara, is in plain sight for the others. Richard is surprised when it darts around, vibrant and excited, poking at Jeanne, taunting her because it knows the true identity of the instigator. The gummy worm shrinks and backs up.

"No," Sara whimpers, "That would not be cool at all." She grabs the blanket from the end of the couch and wraps it around her head as if it could protect her.

Jeanne stands up. *Really, bitch? Who do you think you're playing with? This was my house first and*

*I'll do what I want.*

Richard and Elizabeth can hear her even if Catherine and Sara can't. Richard struggles to get at her, but Elizabeth keeps him away from Jeanne's anger. Her negativity spreads itself out, infiltrating spaces that are not taken up by the girls' natural state of happiness. It mixes with Sara's aura, allowed in and strengthened by the terror that hangs like fringe on the edge of her spirit.

*Well, look at that,* Jeanne says. *The cheeky bitch was right. Fear is my friend. It makes me feel like Popeye. Like I just ate my spinach.* She turns her attention back to the kitchen and reaches out a hand. The energy around the chair begins to wobble.

*That's enough.* Richard leans forward, but Elizabeth stops him. He jolts backward as if he has hit a wall.

*Catherine's got this. No worries. Drink your wine and watch.*

"Well? So that's it? All of that build-up for nothing?" Catherine stands up, looking taller than she really is. "I was ready for a show. This seems about right though. Disappoint me in life and then again in death. Typical."

Richard's shoulders slump, but Jeanne is frozen. She has a grey arrow poised and pointed at the kitchen chair, but she and it are paralyzed by the protective red that is emanating from Catherine's solar plexus. It has locked Jeanne's milky form and her ugly energy in a cage.

Seconds later, the spell is broken and Jeanne collapses in midair. Catherine's radiance claims the room, leaving Jeanne's shrunken form to thrash about in its own pool of blackness. The women go back to their television program, silent and relaxing on their pillows, as if nothing had just happened.

The light in the middle of the front door is gone, along with the wine. Jeanne writhes as if in pain and Elizabeth frowns when Richard growls, *That creature is never going to get near my daughter again.*

\*\*\*\*\*

The space around Jeanne has transformed into a smoky hate that expands with each passing day. Elizabeth and Richard try to reason with her, reminding her that she can't take the doll with her when she crosses over, and reassuring her that Adam will soon grow tired of playing with it. *It's a good size toy. It fits really well in the seat of his truck. And he only uses it when his sister is at school because he misses her and wants someone to play with.*

Jeanne crouches in corners, her neck bent. She growls in response to their advice and bares her gnarled teeth. Sometimes Catherine and her family can hear her guttural sounds, but they are explained away as the neighbor's cats fighting.

Adam has begun having trouble sleeping again. He complains to his mother that there are people in his room and that they bother him in his dreams. He cries out, "No, no, no! Stay 'way lady! Dat's Becky's doll! Stop it! Stop it!"

Richard lingers, combing his grandson's bright

aura with his own radiant blues.

Elizabeth is with Maya, who is not well. When she is woken up by her brother's shouting, she coughs uncontrollably. "Don't lady! Stay 'way!" Adam whines and Maya stirs, unable to catch her breath before she starts hacking away again.

Catherine runs the shower hot in the bathroom. The steam is as thick and heavy as what Jeanne has cloaked herself in. "Oh my poor little monkey. What is wrong, Angel?" Catherine rocks her as Maya clings to her chest. Elizabeth is by their side, enveloping them in a blanket of warm blue.

*****

With everyone occupied, Jeanne slinks away into Rebecca's room. She studies the lavender walls and sheer butterfly curtains. When her son Anthony was younger, he'd lie in his bed and stare at this ceiling until his eyes closed.

Jeanne remembers climbing a ladder and carefully placing tiny glow in the dark stars and planets on his ceiling. She positioned them just like the photographs in his science book. She thinks of how Anthony's eyes lit up after she shut off the lights. He had his own night sky right inside his room.

*Neither of my sons grew into men that I could be proud of.* She kicks at a toy on the floor and sighs. Her raspy breath sounds like her mother's did at the end of her life. She allows her memories to erase the humanity that had crept back in.

*How many Barbies does this spoiled brat have?*

*This one looks like the wife Anthony beats, and this one...* Jeanne's thoughts trail off and she extends a hand. A blond-haired doll obediently floats up toward her spindly fingers. She turns it around in the air, examining it closely. *If it had some meat on its bones, it could be my Anna Maria.*

She flips it around a few more times and thinks about popping its head off before reconsidering and bringing it closer. Murky browns and blacks converge upon the doll's slender torso, dulling the glitter that speckles her evening gown.

*Any port in a storm, I guess.* Jeanne shrugs her shoulders and cradles Anna Maria's substitute. She sings, mouth open, her lonely voice a quiet wail. "Anytime, day or night, I can count on you. My friend, my love, always true blue..." Jeanne rocks slowly, her back small, like a young child caring for her favorite baby doll.

\*\*\*\*\*

Rebecca stirs once Jeanne's song finds its way into her dreams. Caught in the twilight state, where dimensions meet and unlikely connections are made, she mistakes Jeanne for her little sister when she looks over the railing of her bunk bed.

Maya has made a habit of escaping from her crib each morning and heading straight for Rebecca's room. Sometimes she climbs into the bottom bed and calls out, "Sissy?" Then she waits for her big sister to come and cuddle her.

Most of the time though, she plays with the dolls

she finds lying on the floor.

When Rebecca spies Jeanne, made vulnerable by the fantasy of being reunited with her doll, she says, "Maya?"

Her voice is tiny, like the pop of a bubble. Jeanne releases the doll and it drops to the floor. When she looks up, Rebecca recoils at the wrinkled skin, puckered like rotting fruit. The hag's burlesque lips grin at her and the blackened eyes bore through her soul, somehow not at all blind.

Rebecca falls back on her pillow, heart pounding. Fear has taken the air from her.

\*\*\*\*\*

Jeanne focuses hard, her intention to remain visible. She waits patiently until Rebecca peeks back over the side of the bed.

When she does, silent tears stream down the little girl's face. Jeanne locks eyes with the innocent whose vocal cords are terrified into paralysis. Then she ties the child's neck with an ominous grey lasso that keeps Rebecca's head still and forces her to stare at the decaying image of a dead woman.

Jeanne moves toward the bedroom door. *Now, this is what I call fun.* She draws energy from the thick pea-green fear that leaks from Rebecca's aura when she makes the six-year-old watch her push the door shut.

\*\*\*\*\*

Catherine is thirsty after the steam bath she had

with a now fast asleep Maya, so she heads to the kitchen for some water. As she passes the bathroom that is across from Rebecca's bedroom, she pauses to check her haggard appearance in the mirror. Most of the steam has cleared, but remnants of the heavy air still drift out into the hallway.

The glass reflects back tired eyes and crazy hair that makes a punchy Catherine giggle. She is about to continue on to the kitchen when she notices that Rebecca's door is moving. Afraid that the strains of single motherhood have finally taken their toll on her, she turns around to look at it with her own eyes. Rebecca's door closes, then opens again.

Her adrenaline races, replacing her initial surprise with maternal love for the little beings she swore to protect long before any of them ever took their first breaths.

Catherine isn't sure who she is talking to, but it doesn't feel like her father. "Are you kidding me?" She reaches out and grabs the moving door.

She hears Rebecca call out weakly, "Mama?" The fear in her daughter's voice infuriates Catherine and she steps into the room, indifferent to the fact that she cannot see who the enemy is.

"Do not *ever* go near my babies."

*****

Elizabeth and Richard had rushed out into the hallway and flanked Catherine. But when she makes contact with the door, it is clear that they are not needed. They jump away, now only spectators of a fight that is not theirs.

Her powerful blues and pinks throw Jeanne backward, away from Catherine and her daughter like an explosion. Each word she utters is a dangerous warning. Each sentence a weapon cocked and ready to fire the second she senses a threat against her children. "If you want to haunt me, that's fine. It's fun for me to watch you exert yourself. But you're *dead*. Got that? This is my house and my rules. Stay away from my kids. It is *not* ok."

Catherine's aura grows and crackles. She speaks truths that are reflected in the band of colors that spread throughout the room, forming a protective bubble over Rebecca's bed and forcing Jeanne out of the space.

Richard and Elizabeth watch as Jeanne's own darkness seems to implode upon herself, nearly suffocating her soulless existence, and making it impossible for her to be near Catherine.

# Chapter 6

It has been a year since Catherine and her family moved into the house, but even before they settled in one place, she was the sole provider and caretaker of her small children. Without the help of a nanny or significant other, her body is screaming out for rest. One Saturday, she finds herself as tired as her kids are after a long morning spent teaching Maya how to slide down their long hallway.

They are napping, so Catherine does the same. At last, temporarily relieved of duty, she can relax. She sleeps deeply on the couch. Her mommy radar is running on low, letting dreams of flying and dancing take over her subconscious. The tiny pattering of feet and the quiet click of the door knob are drowned out by her laughter. Her dream self is spinning with arms open wide, enjoying the field of sunflowers she finds herself in.

A loud clatter rouses her. Still not a hundred percent familiar with the sounds of the house, it takes Catherine a few minutes to figure out where the noise is coming from.

She is searching for the source when she realizes that her son is missing. She runs back in to the living room, screeching his name. "Adam? Adam! Come honey! Come to Mama!"

When she hears a thump in the basement, her heart drops. She flings open the door to the stairs and finds Adam flailing around. Mops and pails, previously hanging on pegs, bang against each step before clattering hard on to the dirty, cement floor below.

His body is strangely tipped forward, as if held

up by an invisible force. He is slapping at the cleaning supplies, trying to fight his way back out into the light.

Catherine snatches him up, knocking things out of the way. A dustpan crashes to the floor instead of her son, and she kisses him all over his head and face. "Oh, my baby! Are you ok?"

Adam nods, his body shaking as he sobs. When his breathing slows, he leans his head on his mother's shoulder, taking his thumb in his mouth. Catherine cries with him, inhaling his scent, having learned the hard way that every moment is a gift. "I love you so much, my angel. I never want to lose you."

When they have both calmed down, she puts a sleepy Adam back in his bed and goes downstairs to clean up. The dustpan is upside down and leaning on a small train she finds lying on its side.

Catherine studies the toy. She surmises that Adam had it in his hand and dropped it as he struggled to keep his balance. She flinches and shivers when she imagines her son's body, still, broken, and wet with dark blood, sprawled out on the hard cement floor.

She shakes her head to erase the image, but she can't let go of the thoughts that nag at her. *Adam knows how dangerous the stairs are and he is afraid of the dark.* But as quickly as the question forms—*How did this really happen?*— it is gone, washed away by insecurities and regret. Guilt about falling into such a deep sleep sneaks in and extinguishes her sixth sense.

That night, Catherine and her mother install a latch high on the basement door, so that no one under five feet tall will ever find themselves in that situation again.

*****

Richard and Jeanne watch as Catherine and her mother work on the lock. He has a black hold on Jeanne's neck, chaining her like an animal while he waits for Elizabeth to come. It pains him to hear his daughter recount her side of the story to his ex-wife.

He knows that what she experienced scared her, but he is glad that she doesn't know the truth. About how Jeanne had led Adam to the stairs. The curious little boy saw the toy train bouncing around in the air and followed it like a carrot on a stick.

If Rebecca hadn't been sleepwalking again, Richard would have gotten to him faster. Sensing the danger, he quickly pushed his granddaughter away from the edge of the bunk bed before she jumped off of it. Away from what she thought was a diving board over a cool, blue ocean.

He shoved her backward onto the mattress and shut her eyes with a soft yellow mask before he rushed to where Jeanne had led Adam. He found them behind the closed door and on the tiny landing.

With one blazing red swipe from Richard, the train flew from Jeanne's murky clutch to the basement floor. She cackled, mouth open, startling Adam so that he tottered. His foot slipped, but Richard caught him with one hand in a golden cradle.

"It's ok Buddy. Grandpa's got you." It was the first time he had allowed himself the title of grandfather, by speaking the truth out loud. The shift was revealed when the same silver lining that defined

Elizabeth's form appeared in the protective grip he had on his grandson.

Jeanne snickered. With his other hand, Richard held her neck and hands in the darkest of vices, but she didn't struggle. Instead, she used her mouth to speak, "You are as bad at this family thing as I am. We are the same, Richard. Don't kid yourself. You are stuck and ugly, just like me." Her grimace contorted and glowed, even in the black of the stairwell.

Adam cried out. With Richard's attention focused on his love for his family, Jeanne's words couldn't touch him. He wouldn't allow her negativity to loosen his grip. He would not let his grandson plunge down onto the hard cement.

When Catherine describes the weird angle of Adam's body—"It was like he was hanging in midair!"—it doesn't bother him to hear her give Elizabeth the credit. "Grandma, I know you were there protecting him for me. Thank you and I love you."

Finally, Richard is able to enjoy the same feeling of selflessness that Elizabeth showed him in both life and death. His grandson is safe. It doesn't matter that the spotlight shines on Elizabeth. She deserves it and he owes her.

Now, Richard turns away from the women he had once hurt and faces the shadow of what he could've become if not for Elizabeth's love. Jeanne thrashes about, panting and snarling.

When he thinks of all the good these souls—his family—bring out in him, a silver beam of excitement weakens her before it pushes her into a corner, like a pile of useless dust.

98

He might've been like Jeanne in life, but Richard vows to redeem himself in death.

\*\*\*\*\*

It is close to midnight a few weeks later, when Catherine is relaxing, lap top open and skyping with her cousin. They are laughing when Catherine hears noises coming from Adam's room. "Hold on a second Sara. I think Adam just woke up."

An electronic toy beeps, and something shuffles around on the floor. "I'll be right back," she says, then jumps out of bed and hurries across the hall.

Adam is asleep and his floor is clear except for a lone dump trucked parked on the Winnie The Pooh area rug in the center of the room. That is Adam's favorite spot. He sits and plays, often talking to the characters that are pictured skipping happily across the small, round rug. "Pooh 'gain? T 'gain? All my friends," he coos happily as he drives cars over their snouts and paws.

Now though, all is as quiet as it should be. *That's strange. Did I fall asleep on poor Sara? Was I just dreaming that I heard something?*

She returns to her conversation, only to be interrupted five minutes later. This time, the noises come from the hallway. "Sara, can you hear that?" Catherine asks. "It sounds like Adam is playing by the coat rack...when he's supposed to be sleeping..." She raises her voice, hoping her son will hear her.

The shuffling and scraping continues, loudly enough that Sara hears it too. "Are you sure that's

Adam?" she asks.

"Oh yeah, it's him," Catherine says. "And he has about three seconds to wrap it up and get in that bed before I come out there..." She turns her head toward the door, so that maybe her threat will scare him back into his room.

*****

*Yes. Please come out here bitch. I can't wait to see what you're gonna do.* Richard and Elizabeth can hear Jeanne's thoughts, but the black fog around her is too thick for them to try and get close.

Elizabeth's hands are raised, palms open and flat, projecting two silver walls that act as barriers in the doorways and keep Jeanne from the kids. They had just walked in on her snooping around Adam's room, drawing in energy from his automated toys while she searched for her doll.

*Betty, this is out of control. If she gets any stronger, she's going to hurt someone. We need to figure this out.* Richard says it while looking for an opening in Jeanne's aura. A rip or a tear that will allow him to get through and contain her.

Elizabeth nods in agreement. They don't need to share their thoughts. They need to get her out of the house.

*****

The girls are having a "sleepover" in Rebecca's room—it's a trial run as Maya begins the transition from crib to bed. Without a roommate for the night, Catherine has the freedom to cyber-hang out with her cousin.

She looks over her shoulder toward the noise in the hallway. "Adam isn't listening, and I can't figure out why," she whispers to Sara. "This is weird. He's such a good kid."

"They all are," Sara answers. "You're right. It is weird."

"Alright then Adam, I'm coming…" Catherine gives him another second to go back to bed, but the noise continues. She grunts when she pulls back the blanket and stomps out into the hallway. "I'll be right back Sara. I need to find out why my son is being rude tonight," she calls out to both of them.

Earlier that day, Catherine had gone to the supermarket. The "Go Green" movement had started, so she began using shopping bags made of recycled materials, confident that she was contributing to a better environment for her children and grandchildren.

After she unloaded the groceries, she had stuffed the empty bags into one large one. Then she placed them by the front door so that she would remember to put them in her car the next time she went outside.

The hallway is dark except for a dim glow cast from her bedroom lamp and from Adam's tiny night light. Still, the scene before her is as clear as if the hallway were well lit. The stern line of her mouth morphs into a surprised *O*.

She stumbles backward but grabs the molding around her bedroom door. Knuckles white, she watches as the one large grocery bag "walks" across the hallway. It shuffles from side to side, inching its way forward, and twitching as if an animal is trapped within the folds of the stored bags.

"Oh my God," she whispers. She quickly flips through mental files, years of experience and knowledge, searching for an answer that will explain what is happening.

*****

Jeanne twists the bags with gnarled, shadowy black fingers. She grins when vomit-green dots as tiny as pinpoints, freckle Catherine's aura. *There it is,* Jeanne says, *I knew you had to be afraid of something.* Her words are as slurred and indistinct as her form has become.

Elizabeth can hear her, but she keeps her hands up. She will remain the wall between Jeanne and the babies. She blocks Jeanne from her thoughts. *Richard, don't get involved. Conserve your energy for the big things.* Then she nods at Catherine. *Her higher self knows what to do, even if it's hard.*

Her granddaughter is growing from the inside out. Bright violet alignment expands, devouring the green speckles Jeanne had celebrated only seconds before. Her body and her life force are outlined in silver when she takes a deep breath and steps toward Jeanne.

Catherine winds up and kicks the bag over. Her determination to protect her house and family shows in the way that Jeanne and her dirty energy fly into the tiny corner between the coat rack and door. Catherine's inner self holds her there, and Elizabeth watches Jeanne melt.

The colors that had just loomed, lurking and waiting to engulf an innocent, had seemed so powerful, so impenetrable. Now, they slowly dissolve into happy, ping pong balls that bounce away from Jeanne and into Catherine's bubble of light and love, as if they belonged there the whole time.

Elizabeth lowers her hands when the fractured skeleton in front of her shivers. It is curled up in the fetal position, unable to defend itself. *I'm sorry,* Jeanne whimpers. *Please help me.* Chalky browns and greys drown out her bogus regret and reveal her manipulation.

Elizabeth shakes her head no and relaxes. There is no fear here, no place for Jeanne to draw on for energy. A sickly yellow stripe of longing leans toward Adam's room. It hangs there listlessly when Jeanne raises a bony hand, its flesh eaten away by her own self loathing. *Anna Maria. Help me,* she pleads.

*****

Catherine waits for an animal to scurry out of the bag she has just kicked over. *What is in there? A mouse? A squirrel? One of the neighbor's cats? What if it's a mouse or a squirrel? What do I do then? Do I catch it? Do I kill it? Oh my God. How do I do either of those things?*

The bags are still. One of the smaller ones has slid out, revealing nothing but more bags and empty space when she kneels down to peer inside. She stands again, so she can nudge them one more time with a toe. *Did I just imagine that entire scene?*

"Catherine? What's happening?" Sara's voice is hard to hear over her pounding heart.

"One sec, Sara. Sorry." Her voice does not shake like the rest of her body does.

With one deep breath, Catherine thinks of her children and picks up the bag. She turns it upside down, dumping everything out of it. Her knees are slightly bent, locked in fight or flight mode, until she releases nothing but more bags. She kicks at the pile and steps back, braced for something to attack her. Still nothing. *If I had brought an animal in, I would have seen it when I unpacked the groceries.*

She shakes her head. "I think I have officially lost my mind," she says to herself. Then she chuckles. "Sadly, I would rather lose my mind than find an animal in those bags." She packs them back up and stands them next to the door.

"Cath? I can hear you talking, but I don't know what you're saying! Are you ok? Is someone in the house? Should I call 911?" Sara cries out.

"I'm coming Sara. I'm ok." Catherine returns to the bedroom and her conversation, but for the rest of the time, she jumps at every creak and sigh the house makes.

\*\*\*\*\*

Richard and Elizabeth are staring at Catherine's front door. In the center of it, at a point just above Jeanne's head, the swirling white light is back, bigger and brighter than before.

*Good for you, Richard!* Elizabeth coos. *You're almost there!*

He smiles, but his happiness falls short of being true when green speckles suddenly appear around him.

*Trust Source.* When Elizabeth strokes him, it is hard not to succumb to her logic. *Catherine and the kids will be fine. She vibrates so high that Jeanne can't affect her. Once you break this attachment and release your guilt, you will find that there is so much more for you between both worlds. You can visit whenever you want. Just let it go.*

He breaks the connection and strides over to Jeanne. A sliver of black goo finds its mark and quietly slithers up to Richard's green fear. When Jeanne uses it to sit up, he ignores her. Instead, he grabs her head in a grey vice.

His eyes are suddenly a projector, replaying images of Catherine's power in a smoky haze outlined with a parental pride that glows electric blue. Jeanne flinches, but he holds her still and forces her to watch. To reexperience her battles with Catherine.

When it is over, he releases her. Jeanne shakes her head and buries it in her arms, peeking up at him from eyes as thin as slits. They are dark, like the thick, clotted blood that drained from Richard's body after he sliced open the dialysis shunt in his wrist and killed himself. It had taken less than three minutes.

*Look at what my daughter did to you.*

He stands his ground when she hisses at him, her humanity finally lost in the spittle that she sprays into nothingness. Her face comes out of itself, a second grimace, attached to a phantom skull by only a few brown threads. It twists evilly.

*Anna Maria,* she whispers. She sounds like a snake, but weak, without enough venom to back up her tone.

*Look behind you,* Richard tells her, and points at the portal. It has opened much wider now, and colorful sparks of light show the way to the real party.

Jeanne looks, but turns back to Richard, snarling. *She can't see anything but the front door,* Elizabeth explains. Then she asks, *Do you feel that?*

Richard nods, but he fights the urge he feels to move toward the light. Its draw is more hypnotic than the alcohol he constantly craved when he was alive. He locks his transparent knees, determined to stay with Catherine a little bit longer

Elizabeth takes his hand. This time when they connect, their colors burst with a radiance they haven't experienced till now. *It's always been there Richard. You just weren't ready to see it. And I doubt Jeanne ever will,* she reveals.

Richard's orange pity flickers for Jeanne. The fallout of his and Elizabeth's linked vibration flies at her. It leaves tiny holes and pockmarks when its brilliance burns the perimeter of her form. She squirms as her negativity churns, searching for a way to reconnect itself.

*It's time.* Elizabeth says.

Richard looks at Catherine's bedroom door. *I understand. And I'm not afraid. But what about this?* He gestures at Jeanne.

Elizabeth's mouth twitches. *Part of letting go is trusting our true selves to know exactly what to do.*

*Trusting yourself is trusting Source, since we are all pieces of The One.*

Richard takes the outline of Elizabeth's face in his hands and kisses her wispy, silver forehead. Her advice is illuminating. He receives it with clarity and relief. His epiphany blends easily with the affection that illuminates the air around them, like a fourth of July celebration.

He goes into Adam's room. With a flick of one finger, he opens the storage compartment of Adam's favorite truck and removes Anna Maria.

Richard guides the doll out into the hallway, smiling while he thinks of the joy it brought to his grandson. How Adam drove around the house with it, pretending that his sister was next to him as a passenger.

Anna Maria floats by Elizabeth and levitates in front of Jeanne, who is now a misshapen smudge shoved into the corner of the hallway. She lifts a weak hand to grab her doll, but Richard moves it away.

*Nope,* he says. *This comes with a condition. If I let you have what you want, you have to promise to leave my family alone.*

Jeanne's face resembles a creature who has been starved for quite some time. She nods enthusiastically. Behind her, the shadow she is now possessed by, shakes its head no, rejecting the deal and brandishing its evil like a sharpened sword.

Richard's aura glows a vibrant blue, almost matching Elizabeth's. He thinks of his daughter and grandchildren. *They will be okay.* The portal has not only opened for him at the end of Catherine's hallway, but one has opened in his mind as well, allowing him the ability to see the big picture.

*That's great, Jeanne. I'll take care of everything.* They both ignore the dark presence that is nudging her, desperately trying to get her attention. *Just follow my directions the same way you did when you wanted to move things.*

The pale, buttercup yellow ribbon of hope is back. Richard watches it slowly emerge from Jeanne, but it cannot wind around her without passing through the shadow that stains it with a heavy green. The shadow hacks at the ribbon, trying to shred it, but her hope pushes past. It trudges slowly through the hollow blacks and browns as if searching for the cure to what ails it.

*****

*We kept this from you for your own good, Jeanne. I hope you understand.* Richard's voice is garbled noise, bent and warped by the intensity of Jeanne's emotions. She chants as her excitement builds. *Anna Maria! Anna Maria! My love! Anna Maria! Come to me! I finally have you back!*

Suddenly, Elizabeth's hand is in front of her face, waving at her. *Jeanne! Time to focus! You know how it works!* Jeanne nods.

With an unsteady wobble, she maneuvers her body into an upright position. She finds herself eye to eye with Anna Maria, whom Richard has trapped in a red cage.

His voice is steady, calm like it was when he

trained her once before. It soothes Jeanne and the sharp prickles in her back subside. *Relax. She's right there. Tell me,* Richard says. *Tell me what you really want and how much you want it.*

Jeanne smiles uneasily. She has reverted into the forlorn little girl desperate to be with her only friend. Their adventures and their comradery are familiar medicines. They enter her bloodstream easily, warming her like a comfortable sweater. She nestles back into it, as if their conversations had always been real. As if Anna Maria's voice had not been an illusion, a much needed mirage on her lonely island.

*I want my doll. I want my Anna Maria. I don't ever want to let her go again. I love her so much that if I could crawl into her skin, I would.*

The cage around the doll disintegrates. *You've suffered enough, Jeanne. Come on. Come close. I'll help you get just what you want.*

\*\*\*\*\*

He beckons her but thinks of Catherine and the kids playing in the yard, smiling and hugging each other, completely at peace. He lets his adoration for them take over the hallway, spinning and building excitedly with new found clarity.

The shadow behind Jeanne is poking her with razor sharp nails, ripping at her energy, desperate to regain her attention. Richard smiles at his former student. He marvels at her ability to ignore the distraction and stay fixed on her intention.

When Jeanne extends her arms, ready to receive

Anna Maria, he swipes at her murky energy. He does so precisely but gingerly, like he is avoiding getting his hands dirty.

The shadow resists. It claws at the air, slapping away the positivity that Richard has infused into the hallway. His love for his family illuminates the space then expands and burns the dark's defenses.

In a last-ditch attempt to gain more strength, the black form reaches for an electrical outlet like a thread worn cobweb stretched as far as it will go. It looks to suck power from the electricity and reclaim its hold on Jeanne.

Richard ignores Jeanne's internal struggle and considers the two things he loves most about his daughter. He humbly acknowledges that her smile and her creativity were his small genetic contributions to a potentially big life. Instead of fighting Jeanne off, Catherine should be using her energy to foster her gifts and share them with the world.

In one motion, he shoves Jeanne into Anna Maria. The shadow, still connected to her like a deformed appendage, has no choice but to follow. With a loud suction cup pop, it is jerked away from the wall.

"What was that?" Catherine asks the question out loud as she comes running.

Richard smiles at the doll. *You're welcome, Jeanne. You said you never wanted to let her go. You said you loved her so much that if you could crawl into her skin you would. I didn't make you crawl. But you're in her skin anyway,* he says dryly.

When he releases his hold, the doll falls to the

floor at Catherine's feet. Richard is dragged toward the portal. He searches for Elizabeth, but she is gone.

*When can I come back? When can I see them again?* He asks the swirling light. It is shimmering, its allure now impossible to resist. He sees the outline of Elizabeth, waiting, waving to him, ready to meet him on the other side.

He turns back to his daughter. Her eyes, the eyes with enormous depth and insight into love, are staring right at him.

*She takes after her grandmother.* He reaches out to touch her, more gently than he ever did in life. The silver lining that is finally a permanent outline for his own form, encases Catherine's in a brief hug that reveals Richard as Adam's protector.

Their reunion provides a clear channel, its frequency strong enough to connect the dots in a flash before he is finally whisked away.

## Chapter 7

"Daddy?" Catherine blinks and he is gone.

The silver thread between them breaks, carrying away the negative images of what her father once was.

Her sixth sense forces its sleepy eye to remain open, to stay awake just a few seconds longer. Clear and forgiving, it easily fits the pieces of the puzzle together before logic and doubt can creep back in and blur the truth.

The angry monster she had lived with is transformed into an imperfect and wounded man, his only perceived power over his life revealed in anger and abuse.

She smiles at the knowledge that he is not suffering in some imaginary purgatory that someone made up. That he has released himself from the prison in which he confined his soul.

She absolves him of his sins against her when she realizes her anger and disappointment were no match for his. He had been the judge and jury all along. He was the only one who could impose or lift his sentence for atrocities committed in life.

Catherine spies the doll lying on the floor and the veil that has been lifted suddenly drops. She is back, once again firmly rooted to her individual reality—a tiny scene within the bigger picture that our true selves create and play within.

Ever changing and always evolving, its Earth-bound players are only concerned with their own roles, blind to the fact that their thoughts and actions are drops in an ocean. Each one not only makes up the whole of this existence, but they ripple out to affect everyone and everything else.

She remembers how the doll floated in the air before it fell at her feet. Although her first instinct is to get rid of it, she is hesitant to touch it. *What if it moves again?*

Catherine shudders when she thinks of how much Adam loved to play with it. How he would talk to it like it was Rebecca.

Finally, she takes a deep breath and picks it up, really looking at it for the first time. She scrapes at the ruby red paint on the mouth until she reveals the pale pink lips that have been painted over.

The damage and neglect the doll has suffered is obvious in its scorched blond hair and partially melted head. The ears are heavily duct taped, as if its owner showed some mercy by protecting it from harsh words or unwanted noise.

Dark black and blue smudges pepper the arms and legs like it had been beaten. Her back and part of her plaid dress are also burned.

*Who could treat something they loved so badly?* she wonders. *Unless they never really loved her at all...*

"This thing gives me the creeps," Catherine says, her sympathy disappearing along with much of her memory about the events that transpired.

She opens the door that her father has just passed through and takes the toy outside to the curb, where her garbage cans wait to be emptied in the morning. She drops it in one of them, among trash bags filled with crushed cereal bits and dirty diapers.

Anna Maria comes to rest on a soggy cardboard box. Its colorful packaging reveals that it once held the play mat that Maya sat up on for the first time.

The doll's head snaps off, hanging loosely from the neck that held it in place. It is officially irreparable.

In the dark night, with only the porch light behind her, the image is faint, but Catherine sees something sticking out of the head.

*Is that paper in there?* She reaches back into the can and lifts it out. A napkin, torn and stained with tomato sauce, has attached itself to Anna Maria's foot.

Catherine pulls a piece of green paper from the head. "What the...? Money?"

The fragility of the toy is forgotten. She tears the head completely from the body and tosses the torso back into the garbage can. Pieces of hardened putty litter the trash like tiny stones. She unfolds wads of twenties and hundreds.

"Why would anyone put so much Monopoly money in the head of a doll?" she asks the empty street. Only the crickets and the night bugs answer, but in a language she can't understand.

The neighbors are no help. They are sleeping peacefully for the first time in years, unable to tell Catherine how sick Jeanne really was.

How a woman with no real role models who was so traumatized by her childhood had no idea how to raise a family. How as soon as the noise from a house full of boys competed fully with the noise in her head, she drugged them all, so that she could manage her household.

Her son's addictions and her husband's physical limits were mirrors of her own obsessions and powerlessness over what had been done to her as a child. Jeanne's demons never left her. They whispered in her ear, stunting her growth while they helped pass a legacy of mental illness down to future generations.

When the voices in her head told her stories of how dangerous Manny and the boys were, she'd force her entire family out onto the front lawn at gunpoint. She sounded just like Marty when she shoved rifles onto her disabled husband's lap and shouted at him. "Shoot us all Manny! Do it!"

Her husband, weak and vulnerable in his wheelchair, had no choice but to turn the guns on her. To protect their sons so they could go back inside. At least twice a year, he would have to call her doctor to readjust her meds.

Finally, the neighborhood was free. Free to walk by Catherine's house, without fear that they would be shot at. For many years, the kitchen window had held onto the evidence. But it offered no explanation as to whether or not Jeanne had been tormented into evil, or if all along, she had come into the world prepared to play this role. To provide the dark that would allow lights like Catherine's to shine brilliantly.

Jeanne, the damaged child who grew into a

woman saddled with mental illness was finally gone. She had been as big and ugly as the tumor that eventually took over and made her hallucinations worse. Her cancer and schizophrenia became a conjoined second brain, in charge, manipulative, and destructive to everyone around her.

Catherine cannot speculate with understanding. Instead, she talks to the doll that Jeanne had clung to for comfort in both life and death. An attachment that Marty had predicted would finally lead to disappointment. The obsession that would lead to Jeanne's eventual downfall.

"Too much lipstick, looking like you could use a tan, and your eyes. Could you be any creepier? I mean, who gives a doll black marble eyes? You're supposed to be pretty, you poor thing."

She can't hear Jeanne's response through lips, bright and overdrawn, that twist and contort with every tiny scream. "You bitch! Get me out of here! I'm gonna haunt all of you until you beg for mercy!"

Jeanne's ebony eyes pop, exaggerated by the contrast of her pallid skin. Their glassiness reflects back the pity shown by her cousin when he found her dead, and by Catherine in the here and now. Dead time and real time overlap and replay in an endless, slow moving loop.

Suddenly, a smell like rotten eggs and hot garbage takes Catherine and her nose by surprise. If it wasn't so dark outside, she'd be able to see the green smoggy haze winding its way from Anna Maria's head. She'd see it carrying Jeanne's negativity out into the world before being sucked back into its rightful owner.

"Oh my God! Eww!" Catherine drops the doll's head into the muddy, dented can, in an opening between the bags, where it falls easily to the bottom. She tosses in some dirt before pushing garbage over the smell.

"Rebecca's got fifty million Barbies. Adam can pick another doll and ride it around on his truck," she mumbles.

Catherine's step is lighter when she goes back into her house, where all is well, and her family is forever loved.

The best thanks that you can give an author is with a review:
https://www.amazon.com/dp/B014U9T1VK

This book is dedicated to my beloved grandmother, Elizabeth, and my dad, Richard. May their souls be at peace. Neither of them was perfect, but they did the best they could while they were alive. They are always welcome in my home.

Many, many thanks to my beta readers, Ana Cantu and Janice Burpee. Without their insights, this would not be the story that it is.

# CF WINN

is a freelance writer of blogs and short stories. She is the Pied Piper of the unconventional and has often allowed herself to be led to places that few of us know exist. Worlds where eccentricity is the norm and even sometimes embraced.

Her off kilter muses have graciously guided her into the awards arena, most notably, Wordsmitten Storycove for her flash fiction story, "Sunday Drives Done Mojo Style."

**SUKI by CF Winn** has been hugging hearts and healing souls all over the world. Change your perspective. Change your life.
https://www.amazon.com/dp/0615726313

**THE COFFEE BREAK SERIES**, CF Winn's collection of short stories, are wildly popular and are available on Amazon.

Some of the titles include:

**KAFE CASTRO**
http://www.amazon.com/dp/B004SUOUT0

**MOORE THAN MEETS THE EYE**
https://www.amazon.com/dp/B0053ZHMKI

**PGB**
https://www.amazon.com/dp/ B0068WACPM

In between promoting **SUKI,** the author is working on **WHEN DWAYNE DIED**, the sequel to this successful novella. She lives in New York with her brilliant children.

**Visit:**
www.cfwinn.com

Made in the USA
Coppell, TX
21 January 2020

14750502R00072